EARTH
READER

TINA RIFFEY

Paperback-Press
an imprint of A & S Publishing
A & S Holmes, Inc.

ISBN: 0692431527
ISBN-13: 978-0692431528

DEDICATION

This book is dedicated to those who encouraged me to continue to write. May your dreams come true.

TABLE OF CONTENTS

ACKNOWLEDGMENTS

Thanks to everyone who answered all the questions I asked.

CHAPTER ONE

Sara Phillips glanced at the deputy driving then looked out the window as they parked beside the crime scene, an open field. The only information the deputy had given her after showing up at her apartment was that the sheriff needed her. However, that was enough to let her know it was an active scene and not a cold case.

Two sides of the field were edged by woods while another was where all the vehicles were parked and the road bordered the other end. A large group of people stood near the cars, and Sara recognized the gray-haired Sheriff among them.

The deputy pulled into a spot behind the last vehicles, shut the engine off then beeped the horn once. Sara watched as the sheriff moved away from the others and approached the car.

She rolled down the window. "Jacob."

"Sara." The sheriff nodded to her. "Thank you for coming."

"Well, can't pass up the riches, now can I?" She didn't do this for the money.

"Yeah, all two hundred dollars of it." The sheriff laughed before turning serious. "The FBI thinks this guy's a serial killer. We found two bodies here yesterday."

"Surface or deep?" She asked as the sheriff opened her door for her.

"The one was shallow, the other deeper. Looked like

something was digging. Coyote, maybe."

"Well, then I guess I'd better get to it." She slid out of the car and stood. "How'd you get the FBI to let you bring me in?" Law enforcement didn't always believe in what she did. It irked her that no matter how many times she proved herself, there was always someone who didn't accept what she could do. Sometimes that would interfere with a case, and cause a case to go unsolved.

"Just told the agents I wanted an expert to look over the site. The head agent sent for a GPR specialist. He's supposed to be here today too, but I'd rather have you."

"I don't take as long." Of course the Federal Bureau of Investigation would want a Ground-Penetrating Radar specialist to go over the grounds. She had worked with the sheriff though for many years, and he trusted her even over professionals with fancy letters after their names..

"Nope." He gestured toward the group and a tall man that moved toward them. "That's the senior partner, Agent Issaro."

Agent Issaro was at least six foot two with black hair and piercing green eyes. He was definitely in shape; his suit was formfitting and showed his muscular body.

Sara felt a shiver run up her spine and she looked at him more closely as he moved closer. Instincts told her he was a vampire.

In the hundred and twenty years that humans and vampires had co-existed, the government had made many laws to protect both sides. Nowadays, being a vampire was like being black or female; it didn't make a difference in most matters.

The sheriff stepped forward. "Agent Issaro, this is Sara Phillips, the consultant I told you about."

Issaro held out his hand and Sara took it, feeling a jolt of electricity go through her at his touch. This hadn't happened before.

"Ms. Phillips."

"Call me Sara. I don't hold to formalities."

"Then I'm Nick." Nick let go of her hand, his eyes swept over her again.

She figured that he was seeing a mousy-looking woman of about forty in jeans and a tee: brown hair cut short and hazel eyes behind black rims. The top of her head came to just above his shoulders and for the first time in a long time she felt petite. "Nick it is then"

She glanced at Jacob. "So everything's been removed, sheriff?"

"Yes, the bodies were removed yesterday and the graves sifted so it's clear."

"Excellent, then there won't be any interference with the reading. Let's get to work, eh?" She moved toward the torn up ground in the field.

"What exactly do you do, Sara?" Nick asked and fell in step with her, the sheriff following behind. "The sheriff didn't say."

"I read the earth." She stopped and suddenly knelt down by the torn up ground, her hand plunging into the loose dirt. The force of the earth hit her hard, but she was used to the sorting and getting down to business. She did not like what she was being told. The energy surrounding the remains had been feminine, and there were seven distinct signatures. "There are five other bodies here. They've been added over the past six years."

"What?" Nick looked at her.

His look was more of surprise than disbelief which was unusual. "The man's been leaving them here for the past six years. I need markers, Sheriff."

The sheriff made a motion to a nearby deputy. "I figured."

"And there's a man watching from the woods to the left." She told Jacob. The man had a familiar energy about him. "He's been here before, but I don't think he's the killer."

Nick immediately looked into the woods, his eyes pausing as if he saw something. When the sheriff sent some of his deputies out, Nick turned his attention back to Sara.

Sara met his eyes briefly, feeling another almost electric jolt to her spine, before standing. She accepted the markers from the deputy and moved around the field, putting the markers in the ground at intervals. "They're all women."

"How do you know all this?" Nick asked her, his eyes on her face.

"I told you, I read the earth." Sara met his eyes, feeling that jolt again as she did so. This was getting creepy. "The earth talks to me. I know a Native American woman who hears the wind."

"How do I know that you aren't the killer?"

"You don't." She turned to the sheriff. "You going to wait for

3

their GPR specialist or start digging?"

"Start digging. That's why I sent a request to Logan this morning and got two teams." Jacob gestured to the group of people still standing by the cars. "You going to be all right while I get them started?"

"I doubt he's going to arrest me right now." Sara gave Nick a side glance. There was a wrinkle in his forehead and he was frowning. "He's still thinking."

"Right." The sheriff gave her a little wave, then moved off toward the group by the cars.

"I have never heard of such a gift." Nick focused his attention on her. "Were you born with it?"

"No. Some shamans have had similar gifts in the past. Not that I'm a shaman." She made a gesture as if to repel that thought. Controlling one element was hard enough but all four, no. "And it's not always a gift."

"You said you knew someone who heard the wind, so there are others like you?"

Yes, though not quite the same. Earth, wind, fire, and water."

"The elements."

"Correct. Each needs a voice." That's what her friend called herself when asked about her gift.

"Is that what you call yourself? A voice?"

"It's as good as any name." She watched as the two teams picked a marker and started digging. Sadness clung to her. She would never get used to this. "I wish I didn't have to use my gift in this manner quite so often."

"How did you get into this line of work?"

"This isn't my day job," she told him, gesturing to the markers. Drawing blood at the clinic was not as exciting as this, but it was a lot safer. "I'm just a part time consultant."

"Well, a consultant then."

"A serial killer tried to make me his fifth victim."

"What?" His eyebrow raised in surprise as he stared at her.

"He thought he had killed me and buried me in a shallow grave, but I dug myself out after he left and went to the sheriff. I told him what had happened plus what I had learned while in the earth and Jacob went after the guy."

"Somehow, I don't think it was that easy."

4

"It wasn't. The sheriff realized that I couldn't have known all that stuff on my own so he confronted me. I told him about my gift. He didn't really believe me at first of course, but over the years he has. I've also helped the State troopers and the Logan police a few times."

"Is finding bodies all you can do?"

"Nope." Sara shook her head. "The Earth tells me lots of things."

"Can it tell you whether this is his only dumping spot?"

"Ah, so that's why you're here." Sara's tone made it a statement, not a question. "You have other bodies and think these are from the same killer."

"Yes."

"You could be right. One of the bodies here was reburied from another place."

"Can you tell from where?"

"The soil composition was sandy is all I can tell you." Sara paused, a thoughtful look on her face. Faint impressions teased her mind's eye. "And that there were at least two other bodies at that location."

"Oh? Women as well?"

"I think so." Sara said. "It's a very faint echo."

The sheriff stepped up to them. "My deputies didn't find anyone in the woods, but they did find these." He held up a bag that contained two smoked cigarettes. "I'm sending them to the lab with a deputy as soon as they do another sweep."

Before either Sara or Nick could say anything else, the two digging teams gave a yell. They had found something.

"Well, I suppose you should get one of your deputies to take me back."

"By your clothing, it would be back to your apartment, I suppose." The sheriff said.

"Yes." Sara nodded her head. "The clinic gave me today and tomorrow off."

"I'll have Wes take you back then. Hopefully we won't need you again."

"Good...It was a pleasure to meet you, Nick. Hope you catch your killer." She turned away toward the deputy who came up behind the sheriff. "I'm ready."

The deputy, Wes, made a go-ahead motion to Sara before taking the evidence bag the sheriff held. "I'll head for the lab after I drop her off. I have two other bags to take."

"Good," The sheriff said. "Thanks, Sara."

"You're welcome, Jacob." Sara gave a little wave and left with the deputy toward the cars. She could feel Nick's eyes on her and knew Jacob was going to be interrogated later if not now. Sliding into the car seat, she looked back and saw Nick talking to the sheriff. That will be one hell of a talk. The federal agent would probably come by and see her sometime before he left to satisfy his curiosity completely.

She settled back into the seat and watched the scenery go by as the deputy drove her away from the dump site.

This was the fifth time a serial killer had used this area for a dump site in the last twenty years. The last few she had helped find, but the earth had told her of one that had never been found and one that a person like her had found long years ago. This land was large, and most of it was national forest reserve, so the sheriff really didn't have the jurisdiction to be digging up the earth. Nick might be authorized since he was a Fed, but still too much trouble for so little. Animals had found what humans had not.

The deputy pulled into the parking lot of her squat three story apartment building and parked next to Sara's blue car. "You okay from here, Sara?"

"I should be." She unhooked her seatbelt and opened the door. "I hope you don't have a late night, Wes."

Before the deputy could reply, the passenger door window shattered.

CHAPTER TWO

"You alright, Sara?" Wes touched her back, his voice breaking through her shock. "Are you hit?"

"I don't feel any pain, so I guess I'm fine." She was a little breathless. That was close. "Can I sit up now?"

"I don't see anyone." The deputy got out of the car and came around to her side. He helped her lean back up, then pulled on her so she was sitting sideways in the seat. "We need to stay here 'til the sheriff arrives."

"I know." She rubbed a hand over her face. What she really wanted to do was go up to her apartment and curl up in her bed--or take a slug of whiskey, but she knew that neither was going to happen. "I think the shooter just wanted to scare me. Either that or he's a terrible shot."

"Could be both." He paused. "You think it might be the guy you saw at the dump site?"

"Or someone who knows the sheriff calls on me."

"That's a long list."

They both went silent. At least two thirds of the people who lived in Debow knew that Sara worked with the police on the side.

"I'm going to look around. I'll be right back." The deputy moved off toward her building and disappeared around the side.

Sara sat silently, leaning forward slightly so that the door partially covered her. She was still recovering from the emotions her reading had stirred up, and now this. Over the years, she had learned to push aside the emotions and get on with the reading, telling the sheriff what he needed to know. But the emotions lingered long after. She would definitely be having some dreams tonight.

Walking at a brisk pace, the deputy reappeared around the other side of her building. He returned to the car and stood in front of her. "You doing okay?"

"For now. Did you see anything?"

"Nothing."

The gravel beneath her shoes had been whispering toward her but she didn't have enough contact to hear clearly what it was saying. She reached down to grab a handful. That touch told her someone had been at her car, and that someone had bad intentions. He had the same familiar energy she felt earlier. She allowed the gravel to fall back to the ground then looked at Wes. "Someone messed with my car. I think it's the man from the dump site."

Wes opened the back door and grabbed the evidence bags before motioning for her to get up. "I think we should move away from the cars."

"You think there might be a bomb?"

"Never know."

Sara followed the deputy until they were about a hundred yards away. "I think if he were still here he would have blown the car already. If there is a bomb, it's set to explode when I start it."

"Or it could be different people."

"Not a nice thought, you know." But she was sure it was the man from the dump site. Her gift wasn't wrong.

Two vehicles pulled into the parking lot; one was the sheriff's car and the other was a black SUV. The sheriff and Nick got out, and both men moved to stand next to Sara and the deputy.

"There might be a bomb in Sara's car." Wes straightened as another sheriff's car entered the parking lot.

"Sara?" Jacob raised an eyebrow.

"I got a flash of someone messing with my car, nothing clear." Sara shrugged. "Someone with bad intentions. He has the same feel as the man from the dump site."

"Okay. I'll have a tech come. Wes, give the evidence to Don

and he'll take it to the lab with the other stuff he has, then we'll talk."

"Right." Wes headed toward the other police car as the sheriff turned back to Sara.

"Do you think anyone entered your apartment?" the sheriff asked Sara.

"Why?" Did he know something she didn't?

"I don't know if you'll be safe staying here," the sheriff told her.

"One of your deputies can stay in the spare room, you know, like Jackson did when Davis threatened me during the Conner case." She wasn't going to be scared out of her apartment.

"We'll see." Jacob frowned as he looked at her building.

"I'll go with her and check out her apartment while you call for the tech." Nick spoke up as he moved closer to Sara. "Then we can go from there."

"That will work," the sheriff said. "I'll get Wes to look around after I talk to him too."

Nick nodded, then motioned for Sara to head toward her apartment. He walked at her side, his eyes roaming the area as he obviously searched for anything out of place. "Did you sense anything before the shot?"

"I wasn't touching the ground, so no. Sometimes I wish I heard the wind instead of reading the earth; I'd get warnings of these things faster, but it has its drawbacks too."

"Oh?" He preceded her into the building, holding her still for a minute. He scanned the small lobby. It was more of a hallway with mailboxes along one wall and a stairway.

"Yeah, the perp has to be present for the wind to bring knowledge." Sara said. "I wouldn't have had warning of someone messing with my car if I read the wind unless he was there and doing it right then. Although the trees can hold knowledge in their leaves and release it periodically in the wind."

"I can see that it would be problematic." He led her up the stairs to the second floor and took the keys from her hand. There were only six apartments. "Which one?"

"2B." She gestured to the corner apartment on the left. "2C is empty right now 'cause the Robbersons are visiting family in another state, and 2D has a weird work schedule."

9

"So no one would hear if there was anyone breaking into your apartment." Unlocking the door, Nick pushed it open and stepped inside. "Does it look like anything's been touched?"

The apartment was open concept with a kitchen, dinning area, and living room in one big area. To the left was a hallway with three doors which contained the two bedrooms and bath.

"Everything looks okay. Let's look at the bedrooms and bath." She took a step forward, but he moved in front of her and went toward the bedrooms so she stopped and watched him look into the other rooms. He seemed to be taking this seriously. "Okay?"

"Nobody's here and everything seems okay," Nick told her.

"Good." Sara closed the door behind her and moved toward the couch. "I'm going to sit while we wait for the sheriff."

"Okay."

Sara watched Nick pace her apartment. You really couldn't tell a vampire from a human by looks unless you looked real close. The eyes could give them away.

When Vampires revealed themselves over a century ago, people had had a hard time grasping that these ordinary looking people were vampires. Most vampires hold regular jobs and are normal next door neighbors, but what really surprised humans is that while long-lived, Vampires are not immortal.

A knock sounded at her door, and she watched as Nick opened it to let the sheriff in. She straightened on the couch and turned her attention to the man. "Well?"

"I called the tech, and he'll be here as soon as he can. I've got Wes watching your car for now, and after the tech is done, I've arranged for Jackson's brother-in-law to fix anything that has been messed with."

"Good." She paused. While she knew the threat was real she really didn't think the killer, stalker or whatever he was would strike again tonight. "You going to have Jackson stay the night?"

"I'm going to stay the night," Nick interrupted before the sheriff could answer. "I'm going to call my partner and move my vehicle while the sheriff is still here."

Sara and the sheriff watched as Nick left the apartment, then Jacob laughed. "Another conquest?"

"He's curious about my gift."

"I think there's more to it than that." Jacob told her. "He asked all kinds of questions about you."

"Well, he did say he never met anyone like me."

"No one's like you…" the sheriff paused. "You might need more than tomorrow off from the clinic."

"If I do, you can call them and explain. They'll take it better from you."

"You'd think they couldn't function without you the way they carry on sometimes." The sheriff shook his head.

"Well, I could run the whole clinic on my own, you know, since I know every job." She had after all been hired first as a receptionist before learning to be a phlebotomist and aide.

"Ten years is a long time, Sara. Perhaps you should find another job or be on my consultant payroll full-time. You're a damn good investigator, girl."

"Thanks for the offer, Jacob, and I'll think about it. I'm tired." Ten years was indeed a long time, but she did enjoy the time with the clients.

"I mean it, Sara." The sheriff paused as a knock sounded, and he moved to open the door to admit Nick. "Everything taken care of?"

"Yeah. My partner will stop by in the morning with a change of clothes for me and I pulled into a parking space. Your deputy taped off her car."

"Good," the sheriff said. "The digging crew will wrap up soon with the two they're working on. Since it will be dark in a few hours, I'll start them off fresh at sunrise tomorrow with the others before meeting you at the office."

"Fine." Nick nodded. "Good evening, Sheriff."

"Good evening, Sara, Agent Issaro."

Nick closed the door behind the sheriff and flipped the dead bolt. He turned to look at Sara. "I don't think you should be alone for the next few days."

"The sheriff said something similar." Sara rubbed her hand over her face with a tired sigh. "He thinks I should take a few days off work."

"I think that would be a good idea." Nick moved into the living room area and sat in a chair. "How would you like to follow two FBI agents around for a few days?"

"You asking or telling?"

"A little of both." He relaxed into the chair. "One of the bodies removed the other day was only days old, so Elliot and I are going to stick around for a while since I believe the killer is still here. Whether he's the one after you, I don't know."

"But it is suspicious since this stuff happened after the bodies were found."

"Right. About that." Nick paused. "The sheriff said you've been helping them out for the last ten years."

"Him and the Logan police." Sara told him. She knew he had interrogated Jacob after she left. "I also helped the Staties a few times as well."

"What else can you do besides find bodies? And what exactly do you do?"

"I'm like a medium, I suppose, except that it's the earth that talks to me instead of people spirits. True shaman have all four of the elements and can do wonderful things, but those of us with only one can only read that aspect and have limitations specific to that element. My level of reading varies with the access I have."

"So there are downsides?"

"Yep." Sara nodded. Are there ever. "The major one is if you're not compatible, you can go insane and kill yourself or others."

"Compatible how?"

"Understanding and separating what is you and what is not." Sara smiled. "Voices in your head are not always a good thing, right?"

"I see what you mean."

"Also, I can't read through concrete, asphalt, or brick. I can get flashes through gravel, but it won't be a clear reading. I'm not sure why." Sara shrugged. "But I think it has something to do with coming in contact with more than one element. I already told you a limitation for wind; there are others for each aspect."

"So artificial or man-made block the signal as it were, but natural materials only mute it?"

"Right" That was a simple way to look at it. "The more contact or access I have the better the 'signal'."

"How did you get this gift?"

"That's a story for some other time." Sara rolled to her feet and moved to the kitchen. That was a can of worms she definitely didn't want to open. She wouldn't be able to keep her emotions calm. "I'm hungry."

"I still have questions." He warned her.

"I know and I'll answer at least some of them." She opened the refrigerator and pulled out a pizza box. Grabbing a bottled water as well, she closed the refrigerator and moved towards the microwave. "I don't have the answer to everything."

"Who does?" He paused as he notice what she was about to eat. "That's not very healthy."

"No, but it tastes good." She took a sip of water. "Is your partner a vampire too?"

"No, quite human."

Sara gobbled down one piece, then finished a second slice of pizza before walking back to the couch. She threw herself down and stretched out, her free hand going for the remote. "The news should be on soon."

Half her mind was on the TV, but she was thinking about Nick with the other half. He was different than the vampires she had met at the clinic and around town. There was something almost electrical about him as though there was a psychic current running under his skin that connected with her whenever she was near him. Her gift told her if the person in front of her was a vampire since they were connected to the Aether through the Earth aspect, but never anything like this feeling.

Rubbing her face again, she dragged her attention fully to the TV. The anchor talked about the activity at the dump site. At least there were no closeups and they only had vague imaginings about what was going on. She groaned silently when the anchor brought up that the area had been a dump site before, and she just knew Nick would ask her about it so she jumped right in.

"Yes, I helped them find the bodies then too. It was eight years ago, and three bodies found buried in the woods about a half mile away." She forced out in a rush, "All women, strangled. The sheriff shot the man."

"I'll still want Elliot to look at the file," he said in a mild voice. "So that makes three dump sites you've helped with."

"I've found other bodies." Unfortunately, she mostly used her gift that way instead of a more positive way. "A husband kills his wife, buries her in the backyard so the sheriff calls me after he gets a search warrant. A dealer buries his stash so I get called, again after he has a search warrant. A kid lost in the woods and the search party didn't find him? Send me with a deputy."

"That sounds full-time."

"The sheriff only calls on me if he can't handle it the normal way or there's a time crunch. It's hard to explain in a report what I do, you know. He'll have your GPR specialist go over the rest of the field so he can put that in his report if you haven't called him off."

"He had just arrived when we left. That field is visible from the road. Is that road rarely used?"

"It used to be a major road until the new freeway was put in seven years ago. Some truckers still use it since it shortens their drive by a few miles, but yes it's rarely used, especially at night."

"So a person could move about there without detection." Nick stated.

"Most of that land is national reserve, but there are a few houses out that way. Kester County is mainly rural, you know."

"I've studied the maps."

"The one eight years ago, he hid out in the abandoned cabins of the Ryder Inn, just outside of town. Of course, they're not abandoned now, but they're still isolated and readily available."

"I'll have the sheriff send some deputies to check that out." He commented.

"He probably already did that when the bodies were first found."

"I'll see tomorrow." He paused before speaking again. "How much do you know about vampires?"

"The basics, what is taught in school and a little more about your feeding habits." She looked at him. "I work at a clinic, you know."

Vampires lived in daylight, were not afraid of religious symbols, and didn't go around killing people for their blood. The clinics took care of the blood need, and Companions took care of the physical and emotional.

"Then you know about Companions, but not our 'mating system' as you humans refer to it."

"I know that Companions are temporary lovers, and that you vampires can have several, sometimes at the same time. But all they say in school is that vampires only have one mate in their lifetime."

"Mating is a private thing to us. Our mates are the other half of our souls." Nick paused as if deciding something before he gave a little nod. "When we meet our soul mates, we know it instantly, but we have a hard time giving up the life we know to the unknown. The intensity and rush of the new emotions can be scary."

"Humans sometimes feel the same way."

"According to our lore, each soul has two parts." Nick told her.

"Male and female?"

"There is no gender to souls. Physical form doesn't matter..." Nick paused as he shifted in the chair. "Each part of the soul is given a body, though not always at the same time. Once the halves find each other, they are never parted again, not even by death. That's what lore tells us. Real life can be somewhat different."

"Ain't it always?" Sara wondered if this was some form of quid pro quo.

"Always." He smiled. "If the soul mate is human, the vampire courts her."

"With the intent to change her into a vampire?"

"No." Nick shook his head. "Mates share blood, yes. Drinking some of my blood periodically will keep my mate with me for my lifetime."

"They teach us in school that vampire saliva has healing properties, but that transfusing vampire blood can be deadly."

"It is, but drinking it can extend life if used properly. Soul mates can share blood, but if a human drinks too much or is not compatible then the human can die. And drinking a made vampire's blood is just deadly to any human, as you are taught." Nick paused. "If you want to know more about the medical aspects, I can get you in touch with one of our healers."

"Maybe later." So this was a form of quid pro quo, Sara thought. She told him a little about her gift so he was telling her a little secret about vampires. Probably hoping she would tell more about herself. "So bonding is done by the blood sharing?"

"Yes. Sex is optional, but it does strengthen the soul bond."

Sara knew he stopped here for her sensibilities, not his own since vampires got a mental thrill from drinking during sex, much the same as draining the human completely.

Emotions played a great part in a vampire's satisfaction; blood by itself only feeds the physical need. It was like the difference between hamburger and steak; one wasn't as tasty as the other.

"You can see, I'm sure, why we keep this private," Nick said.

"Scientists would want to experiment. By letting everyone think you change your mate you keep that at a minimum."

"Well, there are changes, but like I said if you want details I can get you in touch with one of our healers."

"I'm more interested in vampire culture than medical information." Which is why she had joined the clinic since vampire culture was centered around blood as that was their life force. The medical stuff was just incidental to her.

"I saw the book on your nightstand," Nick told her.

"I've been interested in forensic anthropology since I became a consultant." Besides that was human information, and helped with the comparison between human and vampire. "It helps me understand my consulting work sometimes when Jacob explains a case to me."

"So you do more than find the bodies."

"Sometimes." She replied. "He takes me to cold case crime scenes occasionally, and runs through the case with me, then I do my thing."

"You are full of surprises."

"More than you know." She yawned, then stood up. "I think I'll head for my room. You can use the other bedroom or sleep here on the couch."

"I'm not tired right now."

"As you will. I'll see you in the morning." They exchanged nods, and she headed toward the bedrooms.

With all the impressions, emotions, she had picked up from the dump site, she knew she was in for a rough night. The violent emotional energy she had absorbed would be couched in dreams, vivid, violent dreams that came from her deepest fears. This was another downside to being a 'voice', one that caused many a candidate to refuse the 'honor'.

However, that was for later. Right now, her bed was calling her name, and explaining any nightmares Nick might hear could wait until morning.

CHAPTER THREE

Nick's partner showed up just as Sara finished her morning ablutions and was coming out to the kitchen. She let him in at his knock, noticing the suit he carried over his arm.

He was a head shorter than Nick with blond hair, dark eyes, and a stocky build, but what surprised Sara was that he looked to be a teenager. She knew Nick's partner had to be older than 18, but he had a baby face, an innocent look.

"He's twenty-four," Nick said as he took the suit and a small bag from his partner. "Elliot Wayne, Sara Phillips. I'll just get ready."

As he headed toward the bathroom, Sara moved farther into the kitchen. "Did you already eat?"

"Yes," Wayne replied. "The hotel had a breakfast tray out."

"Martha's very proud of that." She opened a cabinet and took out a box of toaster pastry. "Before she took over we used to have to go to the café."

"I had dinner there," Wayne told her. "The food's not bad."

"John keeps it edible." After taking out a toaster pastry packet, she put the box back into the cabinet, then moved to the refrigerator, getting a soda. "How long have you worked with Nick?"

"Four years. His last partner retired or he'd still be working with him." He paused as she took a drink of her soda. "That's not a very healthy breakfast."

"Don't tell me you're a health nut."

"I'm not, but you should start your day right."

"You can ask, you know. I can see the curiosity." Sara said to his continual staring.

"I have a lot of questions about different things."

"I'm not a psychic or a charlatan. I read the earth."

"So what you do is not a form of psychometry or dowsing?"

"I usually don't see images, though I do occasionally when I read through gravel. The earth 'talks' to me, though not always in words. I can't really explain it." She finished off her toaster pastry as he stared at her. It was hard to explain to someone who didn't have a gift of their own. "How do you know about past-viewing and dowsing?"

"The Bureau has a few psychic consultants, believe it or not; and I've sat in on a psychometry consultation. He touched the murder weapon and explained the whole scene which the suspect later confirmed. A year later, a local dowsing witch found a buried kid by following her rods during a kidnapping case."

"Sounds like you get the unusual cases."

"Nick and the section chief pick the cases we follow up on." Wayne glanced down toward the hallway. "I've never seen him like this though."

"Like what?"

"Personally involved." He looked back at her. "Normally he'd let me look after victims and witnesses."

"He's as curious as you about my gift, I think." No one would be interested in her in any other way. Not anymore. They expected things she could no longer give.

"Maybe." Before Wayne could say more to her, Nick entered the kitchen. "All done?"

"Yes." Nick told him. "How were the autopsies?"

"The M.E. wasn't a very talkative man, but it looks like our killer. Both reports should be at the sheriff's office when we get there."

"Good." Nick paused as Sara shoved the last of her second toaster pastry into her mouth and picked up her soda. "You ready to go?"

"In a second." Sara gulped down her soda and tossed the can into the trash. "We're headed to the sheriff's office then?"

"Yes." Nick opened the apartment door and motioned for Wayne to head out first. "We've set up everything to do with the case in his conference room."

Sara followed the two men out, then turned and locked the door. She went down the stairs behind Wayne with Nick coming behind her. They were taking the threat more seriously than she was. She didn't think the shooter had wanted to kill her, just scare her.

When they got to the lobby door, Nick went out first and pulled the vehicle close to the building before Wayne let her outside. Wayne slid into the back while Sara slid into the front seat beside Nick and put on her seat belt.

Once both of them were settled, Nick began to drive out of the parking lot and onto the street. "How long have you lived in Debow?"

"Jacob not tell you that?"

"I didn't ask."

"Mmmm. I've lived here on and off since I was eight, but I moved back twelve years ago this last time." She paused as she turned to stare out the window at the passing scenery. "I had just broken up with my fiancé."

"Sorry if I brought up bad memories."

"They're just memories, neither good nor bad."

"You have your gift then?"

"Yes, but that was only part of the reason we broke up." She didn't want to get into all that right now. Maybe never. Some things never truly healed or were forgotten. "I was still getting used to it at that time myself. It's second nature now."

"How exactly does it work, this gift of yours?" Wayne asked, speaking for the first time since they entered the SUV. "Since you said it's not psychometry."

"Like past-viewing. It's through touch that I receive, but usually it's a burst of knowledge, words or feelings, not images."

"So you touch the earth and it tells you what happened there?" Wayne leaned forward as he spoke. "Or do you ask it to tell you what passed?"

"Both, most times." She turned her head to look at Wayne. "I get a burst when I first touch the earth, but for details I have to ask."

"You have a connection with the earth even when you're not touching it, right?" Nick asked as he pulled into a parking place in front of the sheriff's office. "That's how you knew someone touched your car."

"Well, technically, I'm touching the earth when I stand or walk on the ground, so yes I feel a connection all the time, but it's not clear. Clothing and shoes interfere with clear reception."

"That must be distracting," Wayne said. "I would have a problem concentrating on anything."

"It can be, but concrete, asphalt, and brick cut me off completely so no voice, no connection, usually in a building or on a highway. As I've said before, there are limitations as with any gift."

Before Wayne or Nick could say anything, the sheriff leaned in the driver window. "Morning."

"Morning, Sheriff," was chorused back to him from the three in the SUV.

"The autopsy reports from Logan have arrived. I put them in the conference room." He paused. "Dr. Hutson had to deliver a calf this morning so he's running late, but he said he'd get to the dump site before the M.E. van from Logan will."

"I've never heard of the local vet being the coroner before I came to this state," Wayne commented. "It was funeral directors where I came from who were the coroners."

"Some still are, but some small towns don't have funeral parlors," the sheriff told him. "Before Dr. Hutson, our old funeral director was the coroner too, but he died and the Doc took over. Doc said he'd make sure the M.E.'s investigators sent you a copy of their report as well as to both me and him."

"Good." Nick gestured for the other two to get out of the SUV, and slid out himself when the sheriff stepped back. "Sara mentioned that she helped with a dump site eight years ago. The man hid out in some cabins?"

"I thought of that too and sent some deputies, but no luck." The sheriff moved toward the front door with the others following. "I even ran a check on the one ten years ago, but haven't heard back from that inquiry yet."

Wayne stepped forward and opened the door, allowing the others to enter the sheriff's office first before following them inside. "That area's an active site?"

"There was a dump site a mile in the woods to the west and another a half mile to the east." Jacob paused at the front desk where a female deputy sat. "Becky, did the bomb tech leave a preliminary report here before he left this morning?"

"No. Jackson's brother-in-law said he was taking her car and he'd have it for a couple of days." Becky shook her head, then looked at Sara. "Sorry, Sara."

"Well, I won't be needing it anyway 'til then." Nick had said he wanted her within sight.

"I made you a pot of tea," Becky said as the sheriff turned away toward the short hallway to the left. "It's in the conference room next to the coffee pot."

"Thanks, Becky," Sara replied as she turned to follow the sheriff and the others to the conference room. "I'll need it I'm sure."

The conference room was a sixteen by eighteen foot room with a small oval table in the center with two small rectangular tables against a wall that had a white board on it. It was used mainly for the deputies to have meetings and do their daily logs in when at the office. Otherwise, they used the single interrogation room in the other hallway for questionings, unless it was a witness then they used the conference room.

Wayne and the sheriff both went to the coffee pot that was sitting on one of the small rectangular tables and poured themselves a cup. Nick went to the files on the oval table and pulled one out, handing it to Sara.

"That was the first body found. Wyoming, outside a little town called Heasley. She was kidnapped from North Dakota. Three skeletons were found buried around her, but her grave was shallow as if he didn't care whether she was found right away."

Sara laid the file on the table and sat down in a chair. She ran over the impressions she had gotten from the dump site, pushing both her dreams and her sadness for the victims away. "He cares."

"She's right. The soil here is rocky and takes a lot of effort for any deep digging." The sheriff agreed. "He might have been interrupted in Wyoming."

"A shallow grave was also found in Nevada as well as an empty hole…" Nick shook his head. "So I don't think that's the reason."

Wayne moved to the table and flipped through the two new files before picking one up. "These pretty much tell us what he told me…the woman who was only days old…The ME says about four days according to decomp. She had blunt force trauma to the head instead of being strangled, but she was cut open and the uterus mutilated like the others…He found DNA under the finger nails."

"Did he send it to our lab already?"

"Yes, so in less than 48 hours we should have the results."

With the advancements in DNA and other forensic sciences that the vampires helped bring about in the last thirty years, the long waiting periods for tests was over. DNA was done in 24 to 48 hours, and other tests were generally done in less than 24. Sara just wished that cures were as easy and quick to come by for certain human illnesses.

"The other woman was over a week old by the rate of decomp…" Wayne said as he flipped open the other folder. "She was strangled, but while she was cut open, there was no uterus. The M.E. found scars that he thinks are from a hysterectomy. There was a stab wound to the heart but it was post-mortem, according to the M.E.."

"That's why he killed the second woman; the first one had had a hysterectomy," Sara told them. "He didn't get what he wanted from the first one."

"If we hadn't been looking for that missing kid, he could have kept on using that field." The sheriff shook his head. "I'm going to have to change the patrols and see about adding at least one more full time deputy."

"Don't feel bad, Sheriff. The ones in Nevada were found because a dog brought home an arm." Nick told him. "And the ones in Wyoming were found by lost hikers. If most of the bodies in Nevada hadn't been mummified, we wouldn't even know they were connected to the body and bones in Wyoming."

"So he kills them and cuts them open before taking them to the burial site where he spends an hour or two digging a hole…"

"He makes them dig the hole before strangling them." Sara interrupted Wayne. "Then cuts them open in the hole."

"How do you know that?" asked Wayne.

"The earth told me." Sara met Wayne's eyes. There was no place for disbelief here if they wanted to catch the killer with her help. "Your killer is a blank or a Sinq if you want to call him that. He, himself, may be 'invisible' to me but what happens around him is not. Emotions are energy. The earth absorbs those emotions, and I get the echoes of that energy when I do a reading."

"So you didn't get his energy echo when you read the dump site," Nick said.

"I just got the women's," Sara stated. "The women did the digging though because the Sinq wasn't in the hole until a few minutes before the blood. When he got in the hole the emotions were suddenly cut off, but minutes later blood soaked into the ground."

"Did you recall anything else last night while you slept?" The sheriff asked her. "I know you sometimes dream about the scene."

"It was spring or summer for each murder as the earth was in its time of renewal and growth like now." She paused as she recalled the vague dream she had just before awakening. "The last victim fought him every step of the way. He will have scratches and maybe a bite mark, but where I'm not sure."

"I'll have the M.E. get bite impressions," Wayne said as he pulled out his cell phone and moved away from the others for some privacy. "If she did bite him then that will help ID him as the killer."

A deputy came to the door with a folder, and the sheriff took it from him. After a brief whispered conversation, the deputy left and the sheriff moved back the few steps towards the table. "The DNA results are back from the two women."

"Excellent."

"Neither body came back to anything in either CODIS or AFIS." The sheriff tapped the open folder. "However, Logan PD had a woman reported missing five days ago that might match the one body. Jennifer Kraig, 28. They're getting a DNA sample from the family for comparison. The other body's face is too far gone to run through the Federal Missing Person's data base."

Since neither woman was in either the Automated Fingerprint Identification System or the Combined DNA Identification System, they had not committed a crime nor worked for the government and would be hard to identify unless there was a match somewhere in the missing person data base's limited DNA files.. Sara wouldn't want to be the tech who would have to run that program because even though limited there were literally millions of entries in the system, and it could take days for the program to run its full course.

"Logan PD has a forensic artist," the sheriff continued. "But she's used to doing her drawings from skulls. The M.E. will deflesh the skull and the artist will do her thing. Until then we'll just have to wait one way or the other."

"We only identified half of the remains we found in the other two locations." Wayne said. "Even with a forensic artist there's only a small chance that we'll find out her identity. Especially if she was taken from out of state."

"I know." Jacob sighed. "But we have to try."

"Can I see all the files of the identified?" Sara tapped the file in front of her. "Maybe I'll see something you did not."

Nick picked up four folders and set them in front of Sara. "I've looked at them several times, and each time I get the feeling I'm missing something. Elliot can't find anything either."

Sara nodded and started to flip through the files. She skipped through most of the files' pages until she got to the autopsy and the forensic anthropologists' reports. Each had some added observations in the notes area. With a frown, she reached for one of the unidentified's files and flipped through it. What she found there made her look up at Nick. "Can you get their full medical histories?"

"I can have the files faxed here by tomorrow afternoon." Nick gestured to Wayne who pulled out his phone again and started to text. "What did you find?"

"Each M.E. found scar tissue on the uterus and the forensic anthropologists found certain signs in the pelvis area. I think I know what it means but I want to be sure." She flipped through a file. "All of them seem to have an active professional life, but limited social ties. Anything similar there?"

"They all were active in their church." Nick paused as he thought about that. "All were Catholic. I'll have Elliot get people to interview the priests again."

"I'll have Logan PD do the same at whichever church Kraig

belonged to, just in case," the sheriff added as he moved to the door where a deputy suddenly appeared. The deputy and the sheriff talked in a low voice for a minute, then the sheriff moved back to the table. "Dan said that a reporter from Logan is here. The reporter thinks he has a letter from our killer."

"Why is he here?" Nick asked. "Why not the Logan police?"

"I don't know. The reporter asked to speak with all of us. I told Dan to bring him back."

The deputy appeared in the doorway with a man the sheriff's age. In his hand the man was carrying a large, thick manila envelope. "This is Mr. Moran from The Logan Chronicle."

"I recognize the sheriff, but you two, I don't know." The man commented as he stepped further into the room. "But I'm guessing you're the FBI."

"Mr. Moran, I'm Nick Issaro, senior agent and this is my partner Elliot Wayne. You wanted to see us?"

"Straight to the point...I found this early this morning on my front step." He held out the envelope. "There's a letter in there and a small envelope addressed to Sara Phillips. Since I knew she worked for the sheriff, I came here instead of the Logan police. All I ask is for an exclusive however this turns out."

"You're relaxed about this." Nick noted as he motioned for Moran to set the envelope on the table. "I'm surprised you didn't print this in today's paper, then turn it over."

"Most of my colleagues are at the dump site, including a young reporter from the Chronicle, but I've worked with the sheriff before. Also, I'm a freelancer for the paper so I have more leeway."

"We'll give you an interview before we leave town. Will that satisfy you?"

"Yes, thank you." He turned to leave. "My fingerprints are on file here, by the way."

The deputy at the door stepped aside to allow Moran to pass, then entered the room. He pulled out a pair of gloves and handed them to Nick. "You want to look before we print the envelope?"

Nick slipped the gloves on and picked up the envelope, noting there was nothing written on the outside. He opened it and pulled the contents out before handing the large envelope to the deputy who had slipped on another pair of gloves. As the deputy left, Nick set the small envelope on the table before turning his attention to the letter.

"Is it the killer?" the sheriff asked after a moment of silence while Nick glanced over the letter. "Or an attention seeker?"

"I'm not sure…There's no salutation or signature." Nick cleared his throat, then began to read aloud. "'Did you like my work? Can you understand it? They denied their gift, eradicated it, caused it to return to the great beyond, and they were unrepentant. This is unforgivable.'"

"Sounds like he's on a mission," Wayne commented as Nick paused. "One that he's proud of as well."

"'I thought of moving on when my work was discovered,'" Nick continued. "'but there is still something here I need to finish…'That's all there is. Let's see what's in the envelope addressed to Sara."

"Probably a threat." Sara stood and moved to where she could read whatever was in the envelope with the others. "I get a few of those every time I work for the sheriff."

Nick carefully opened the envelope and pulled out the single piece of paper which had only one sentence. "'Don't interfere with my mission and I won't interfere with yours.'"

"So he is on a mission," Wayne said. "What does he think yours is, I wonder?"

"I don't know." Sara shrugged. "A lot of people in this town know I help the sheriff, but not how I do it."

"Or why," Nick added softly as he looked at her.

"Or why," she agreed, not meeting his eyes. Did the killer know her secret or was he just fishing?

Wayne looked back and forth between them, then turned to the sheriff. However before he could say anything, the deputy appeared at the door and spoke. "There's a mutilated body at the Ryder Inn."

"Is it connected to our case?" Wayne asked

"How many killers you think we have in this town?" The sheriff looked at Wayne. "All this started happening when we found those bodies. What do we have, Dan?"

"I don't know. All Jack Howard said was that his maid found a body in one of his cabins. Wes and the Doc are headed that way."

"Ryder Inn was where the one killer hid out eight years ago, right?" Nick asked.

"Yes. Jack Howard had just bought it and was having it renovated," the sheriff replied. "The killer posed as a workman."

"Can you lead us there?"

"Yes." Jacob nodded to Nick's question. "It's on the edge of the national reserve land on the one side of the dump site. I'll take you the back way there."

"That's fine." Nick looked at Wayne. "Your fancy camera still in the SUV?"

"It's in my bag in the back so yes."

"Good." Nick set the envelope and paper in his hand on the table before looking at Sara. "I'd rather you were not out of my sight."

"Is that your way of asking me to come along?"

When Nick didn't answer, the sheriff laughed. "Put him out of his misery, Sara. I'll be waiting outside."

Sara watched Jacob leave, then looked at Nick. "I told you I've worked with the sheriff on cases. This is no different. I'll even waive the consultant fee, if you like."

"Protection detail, huh?" Wayne laughed, and Nick frowned at him.

"Are you going or what?" Sara asked as she headed for the door. "I can always ride with the sheriff, you know."

"No," Nick barked as he too headed towards the door. "I said I didn't want you out of MY sight, didn't I?"

Wayne laughed again as he followed them out of the sheriff's office into the parking lot. He headed towards the SUV while Nick and Sara stopped next to the sheriff's car where the sheriff stood, waiting.

"Wes and Doc should be there now," Jacob said as he slid into his car. "I told Becky to call the M.E. in Logan so they should be sending a van."

"You said you're taking us the back way?" Nick asked him. "There's more than one way to these cabins?"

"Three different ways, plus hiking through the woods."

"You'll have to show us on the map later... See you at the scene." Nick put his hand on Sara's back and escorted her to the SUV. He opened the passenger door, then closed it once she was in before going around to the driver's side and sliding in himself. "Do all the locals go the back way to the cabins?"

"The locals rarely go to the cabins," Sara replied as Nick started the car and backed out of the parking space. "Except those that work there. They have a reputation of being haunted."

CHAPTER FOUR

"Haunted?" Wayne asked from the back seat as Nick followed the sheriff out of town. "Haunted by who or what?"

"Fifty years ago, back in 1963, there was a triple murder committed there. The cabins had just opened for business the year before by a wealthy businessman called Jason Ryder. Ryder, his wife, and daughter were found murdered in one of the cabins and to this day their murder hasn't been solved. It is said they will wander the grounds until their murderer is exposed. The Inn has changed hands many times since the murders, but Jack Howard has had it the longest."

"So the locals would steer clear of this place." Nick's tone made it a statement, not a question. "What about those who work there?"

"Jack Howard manages the place, but he has two maids, a housekeeper, a maintenance man, and a gardener, all local. But none of which live there or stay there after dark. His wife, his son or daughter runs the front desk."

"So we should concentrate our efforts on guests or strangers, you think?" Wayne asked Nick.

"This could be pointing us in that direction." Nick answered. "If this is related."

"As Jacob said, how many killers do you think are here?" Sara told him. Really. Were they being thick on purpose? "The killer either moved here six years ago or he started taking a vacation here around that time. Otherwise there would be more bodies."

"You could be right." Nick followed the Sheriff's car onto a dirt road that led to a large house surrounded by woods and eight small cabins. "Is this it?"

"Yes." She had always liked the quiet setting here. "Part of the woods belongs to the Inn and there are two cabins deeper in, but most of it is national reserve land."

Nick and Sara slid out of the SUV and moved to join the sheriff who had parked next to the other sheriff's car and a truck. The deputy who was standing on the porch with a man who appeared to be Jacob's age waved to them, and the three of them went to join him and the other man.

"Wes. Jack," the sheriff said in greeting.

"Doc's with the body in cabin one," Wes told the sheriff. "Maria Cortez, the maid is inside. She told me she went in to replace the towels and found the body in the bedroom on the way to the bathroom."

"As soon as she found it, she came to me," the other man told Jacob. "She told me she didn't touch anything, but she did drop the towels."

"Any idea who he is?" Jacob asked.

"Doc gave me this." The deputy held up a driver's license. "John Vernon, Logan address."

"The cabin was rented by a Bob Kirkland," Jack Howard said. "I looked at the license and that ain't him."

"All right. Wes, call Ron and have him come out here, then talk some more to Maria and Jack." The sheriff paused as Wayne joined them, a camera in his hand. "Make sure Ron has restocked his kit. And have Becky run the check on this Kirkland."

"Right." The deputy headed off the porch toward his car and the radio inside.

"You said this dead man ain't the one who rented the cabin." Jacob turned to Jack Howard. "Have you seen him before?"

"No. Kirkland rented the cabin a week ago and would spend most of his time away. He'd get in his car in the morning and not return until late at night. A few times he disappeared into the woods, but mostly he left in his car. He didn't return last night."

"Give Wes the information about Kirkland's car, if you would."

"Of course, Sheriff." Jack Howard turned and went inside while the sheriff turned to the others.

"You think this Kirkland may be our killer?" the sheriff asked Nick.

"Too early to tell." Nick gestured down the porch steps. "Let's look at the crime scene."

The four of them left the porch and headed toward the cabins. Wayne took a picture of the outside of the cabin before they stepped inside cabin one. Kitchen and living room made up the majority of the cabin, and an open door led into the bedroom and bathroom presumably. A few more pictures were snapped by Wayne before they moved together toward the open door at the back.

Just inside the bedroom a man was standing, writing in a notebook, and the sheriff stopped next to him while the others moved closer to the bed and the body lying there.

"Doc?"

The older man acknowledged them then gestured toward the body. "He's been dead at least since last night. I can tell that his tongue was cut out after death, he was stabbed through the heart, and was hit over the head, but you'll have to wait for the ME for anything else."

"This is obviously a secondary crime scene," Wayne commented as he gestured around the clean room.. "Not enough blood."

The room held only a double bed and a small dresser beside the closet, and the two paintings on the wall were obviously mass produced ones. She had never been inside the cabins before but the bedroom reminded Sara of hotel rooms she had been in before, in her other life.

"And no personal items anywhere." Nick paused as he moved to the open bathroom doorway. "There's an ashtray in here with two butts, but nothing else."

Sara moved closer to the bed, her eyes flickering over the body. He was a middle-aged man with brown hair and wearing a bloody tee shirt and torn jeans. There was no expression on his face and his eyes were closed, making her think he had been drugged before killed. His mouth was open with blood on his lips and his tongue lying on his chest.

"He lied about something."

"What?" Nick turned to look at her. "Why would you say that?"

"The tongue." Sara paused. "The killer wanted us to know he lied."

"So this whole scene is for us?" Nick asked her.

"Yes." Of that she was sure.

"Elliot."

"Right." Wayne started to snap pictures as Nick moved back to stand beside Sara.

"I need to go outside," Sara told him.

"Did you pick up on something?" The sheriff asked, looking at her.

"I felt something." Sara frowned as she tried to grasp the faint whispers she had heard earlier when they arrived. "I can tell the Sinq was here, but so was someone else."

"Not the dead man?" Wayne asked.

"I don't think so." Sara shook her head. "That's why I need to go outside and do a reading."

"Okay. I'll go with you." Nick said. "You coming, Sheriff?"

"Yes." Jacob turned to the coroner next to him. "Ron should be here soon, Doc."

"Good. I'll stay here 'til the van gets here, then I'll go back to the dump site. By then they should have all the remains uncovered, and I can sign off on them before they're taken to Logan."

"Excellent." The sheriff turned back to Sara and Nick. "Let's go."

The three of them headed out of the bedroom towards the front door.

"You think the killer might have a partner, Agent Issaro?" Jacob asked as they passed through the living room. "Or another victim?"

"I don't know." Nick and the sheriff stopped just outside the door."When we get more information on this Kirkland, we will be able to speculate better."

Sara moved past them and knelt down to lay a hand on the ground. Her eyes narrowed as a burst of knowledge hit her, and she began to sort through it. She could only read one presence, but there was a familiar echo to the blankness that accompanied that presence. "There was someone else here with the Sinq. The other person was both angry and afraid, but mainly angry. They both came from the woods, went into the cabin, then headed off later back towards the woods."

"Probably to the old fire road," the sheriff said.

"The other person was the man from the dump site." Sara withdrew her hands from the earth, and stood, wiping her hands on her jeans. "I couldn't get a good read because of the Sinq, but the man has definitely been here before so I'm thinking it's this Kirkland."

"Once Ron gets here I'll have Wes check out the old fire road." The sheriff paused. "When we get back to the office, Becky should have the information on Kirkland for us."

"Good. I gather that this fire road is one of the three ways to get here?"

"Yes. It borders where the Inn's land ends and the national reserve land begins which is just a few yards behind the last cabin in the woods." The sheriff gestured behind him. "About two, two and a half acres back, I'd guess."

"Dirt, I'm assuming?"

"Yes. And quite popular with off-roaders so maybe someone saw something. Wes will check that out."

They heard a car come into the parking lot in front of the house, and moments later, two deputies came around the house, headed toward them. One deputy was wheeling a large case behind him, while the other deputy, Wes, was carrying a camera. Both deputies stopped in front of the sheriff.

"Ron," Jacob nodded to the deputy with the case. "this seems to be a secondary crime scene so I want to you pay particular attention to anything that doesn't seem to fit. Also the renter seems to have disappeared."

"Gotcha." Ron nodded. "Will Wes be helping me?"

"Not right away. I want him to check the old fire road first, then check with the off-roaders that usually use it later after the body's been picked up."

"So I'll have him for only a bit then."

"Yes." The sheriff nodded. "If you need more help just have

Becky send Chis."

"Right." Ron took the camera from Wes before going inside.

"You got your phone, Wes?"

"Got it from the car when I spoke with Becky," The deputy pulled out his phone. "You want me to photograph just behind the cabins?"

"Walk up and down the road a bit too."

"Okay. I put a BOLO out on Kirkland's car."

"Good."

The deputy nodded and went around the side of the cabin toward the woods.

Sara knew that BOLO stood for Be On the Look Out for, but she didn't think the killer would have used Kirkland's car for very long if at all so it would probably get them nowhere. "He probably dumped the car, you know."

"Maybe." The sheriff shrugged. "Maybe not."

"The license gave a Logan address, and the one body might be that of a missing woman from Logan," Nick commented. "Perhaps we should pay a visit to Mr. Vernon's address and see if he's connected to Ms. Kraig."

"I can call Logan PD and have one of their detectives meet you there tomorrow," the sheriff said. "I can also see if the detective handling Ms. Kraig's disappearance can meet with you as well."

"Excellent. We can leave tomorrow morning."

"I suppose I'm going as well?" Sara asked with a raised eyebrow.

"Of course," Nick replied. "I did say I didn't want you out of my sight."

"Then Jacob also needs to call the clinic for me."

"I'll have Becky do that." The sheriff smiled. "They won't argue with her."

"True enough." Sara paused as Wayne came out of the cabin behind the sheriff and Nick. "Are we heading back to the office now?"

"Soon, if Elliot's done," Nick said.

"The memory card's almost full." Wayne patted his camera. "All I need is a photo printer."

"We got one. You can give the card to Dan, and he'll print

them up." Jacob gestured toward the house. "Did you want to talk to Jack or Maria?"

"I'd like to speak to Mr. Howard before we go," Nick said.

"All right." The sheriff moved toward the house with the other three following. "Did Sara tell you the history of this place?"

"She told us what happened here fifty years ago." Nick acknowledged. "And that the locals think it's haunted."

"There's been four suicides here since those murders, and guests report weird happenings to Jack. Jack himself has heard things, and he or his wife has called me out many a time for a prowler that I never find proof of. I've learned to keep an open mind."

"Four suicides?" Wayne asked as he followed the others around the side of the house. "You sure they were suicides."

"Yep." The sheriff nodded as he headed toward the porch where Jack Howard was standing. "Each was a guest of the Inn except the first one. That one was the owner's wife."

"Need anything else, sheriff," Jack Howard asked as the others came up the porch steps. "I told everything I remembered to Wes."

"This Bob Kirkland has never been here before?" Nick asked.

"No." Jack Howard paused. "Although he did mention an uncle that visited Debow ten years ago. I didn't pay much attention."

"Do you have any Inn paperwork from back then?"

"There were boxes in the basement when I bought the Inn eight years ago. I can have my son look through them tonight and tomorrow for anything from back then."

"That would help a lot. Thank you." Nick gave Jack Howard a nod before the man headed inside and he turned to the Sheriff. "You said you made inquiries about the killer from ten years ago?"

"Yes, but I hadn't heard back when we came in this morning," Jacob answered. "When we get back to the office, I'll check again as well as see if Becky's got that info on Kirkland."

"Okay," Nick said. "Is your deputy going to turn in the evidence to the Logan Police lab or send it to our lab in Denton county?"

"We've been sending everything but DNA evidence to the police lab like we usually do." The sheriff paused. "You want this evidence to go that way too?"

"Yes." Nick gestured to the steps. "Let's head back to the office. I want to see the info on Kirkland."

"All right. I'll meet you there." Jacob moved off the porch and went around the corner of the house as the other three moved toward the SUV.

"Dr. Hutson told me that the remains they've dug up so far all have broken hyoid bones," Wayne told Nick. "He said they were definitely strangled."

"The remains in both Wyoming and Nevada were the same." Nick opened the passenger door of the SUV for Sara who immediately slid inside. "He say anything else?"

"Just that he didn't see any marks on the ribs so he doesn't think any of them was stabbed in the heart." Wayne opened the back door and slid in. "They still have more to go though."

Nick nodded and closed both doors before going around the SUV and getting in the driver's side. He started the vehicle and backed out, heading toward the entrance of the gravel parking lot. "This town seems to attract killers."

"The land has absorbed a lot of negative energy." Sara said, her eyes on the scenery going by. "There was a massacre here during the civil war, and before that Native Americans wouldn't settle here because of the shadows or ghosts as we would call them."

"Why did you come back here?" Wayne asked. "With all this negativity?"

"I had nowhere else to go." Sara shrugged. Home was home, good or bad. "And it was familiar. Besides the land itself isn't what we would call evil."

"And it was home," Nick said.

"Yes." Sara agreed. "Although only my aunt and one of my cousins still live here."

"The sheriff mentioned that he offered you a full-time job, but you didn't want that." Nick commented.

"I wasn't ready then for a change. I had only been a part-time consultant for a little over two years when he asked the first time."

"But you're ready now," Nick observed. "He said he would ask again."

"He did, and yes I am." Sara sighed. "The clinic has become routine, and I can't stand being bored."

"Don't give him an answer yet," Nick said. "Wait until this case is over, at least."

Sara looked at him, but could read nothing from his seemingly open expression. She knew that Wayne thought Nick was acting strange, but she couldn't figure him out. Nick was curious about her, that she knew, but this she was unsure about. "Okay."

"Good."

"I texted David and asked him to run a check on Bob Kirkland through his network," Wayne said. "He said he'd text me back if he found anything interesting."

"David?" Sara asked.

"David Wells. He's the information and tech guy assigned to us," Nick told her. "Anything we need he gets it for us."

"He's also the head of our office's cyber department," Wayne said. "He has minions do the routine stuff."

"Which is why he works with us," Nick said. "We never do routine cases."

"We're the odd case team of the FBI," Wayne told Sara. "Any case that has anything a bit odd, we get the file, and if Nick thinks it's viable we take it."

"I wondered how the FBI got into this."

"Hikers found that first body with the skeletons, and when it was found out she had been kidnapped from another state, it was given to the local FBI office. They in turn sent it along to us, which caused Nick to have David look for a similar MO. However, it was an agent just back from a conference that told us about the dump site in Nevada. Nick had David put out a notice to notify the FBI if a similar mode of killing happened, and here we are."

"Hopefully we'll catch him here," Nick said as he pulled into a parking space in front of the sheriff's office. "I dread to think how many women he's actually killed."

They all got out of the SUV and headed into the building. Becky was sitting at the desk behind the front counter, and looked up as they entered.

"There's no word yet on the BOLO," Becky told them. "Bob Kirkland is actually Robert Graham Kirkland, thirty-five. He got into trouble ten years ago; an assault charge. Nothing since then, though. I'm still waiting on a call back so we might get more."

"Thank you." Nick led Sara and Wayne to the conference

room, and motioned them in. Wayne headed for the coffee pot as both Nick and Sara moved to the table.

"Things seem to point to ten years ago." Nick looked at Sara. "Perhaps you should tell us about what happened then."

"Four women disappeared from town during a three week period." Sara sat down in one of the chairs, and idly shifted the files on the table before her. She kept her voice calm as she talked about the traumatic event. After all it was over with. "One of the families contacted me because they had heard the rumors that I was psychic. Unfortunately, for me, the killer had also heard the rumors and decided I was his next victim."

"How'd he find you?" Wayne asked. "Was he a local?"

"No." Sara shook her head. "He talked and listened in to some of the gossipers from around town…Anyway, he snatched me from the clinic parking lot and took me to his killing area which in this case was in the woods. I blacked out while he strangled me and when I woke up I was in a shallow grave. The earth told me I was alone with four bodies so I dug myself out and went to find the sheriff."

"Who didn't believe her at first," Jacob said as he entered the room. "I thought she was crazy or in on the kidnappings."

"Good thing the killer was at the dump site when we showed up." Sara said. "Or I'd be in prison right now."

"He said he came back to burn her body," the sheriff told them. "He called her a witch."

"Anyway, he got life in max security," Sara told them. Thanks to her testimony and the overwhelming evidence.

"And as of eight days ago, Richard Graham Mayer was reported dead from an altercation in prison." The sheriff said, "I just got the report back."

"Graham. Kirkland's middle name is Graham as well," Wayne said. "You think the uncle he mentioned is Mayer?"

"I don't know." Nick shook his head. "But I do think Kirkland has been stalking Sara."

"I haven't noticed anyone following me," Sara said. She hadn't felt any unusual eyes on her at all. "But then I've not expected to."

"Elliot, have David get Mayer's visitor log." Nick paused as Wayne pulled out his phone and texted. "And who claimed the body if anyone."

"Right." Wayne finished the text, then grabbed the camera hanging from his neck. He slipped out the memory card and handed it to the sheriff. "Have those printed if you would."

"Alright."

A deputy appeared at the door and the sheriff went to him, handing him the memory card. There was a brief low conversation, then the sheriff turned to the others. "Dan says there's still nothing on the BOLO. He also reminded me that we missed lunch and that it's after 2pm so he called the café. We'll have sandwiches here momentarily."

"I hope John sends along some of his cookies." Sara cleared a space on the table in front of her. "Do you need to visit the clinic, Nick?"

Most vampires needed to feed daily, unless they were very old. Since Nick looked to be in his thirties, he was probably a few centuries old as born vampires aged normally until their twenties.

"I'm not in need right now, thank you."

"Okay." Sara paused. "Speaking of the clinic, did Becky call them, Jacob?"

"Yes, you're off until further notice. Half pay."

"I thought it'd be unpaid."

"Becky worked her usual magic." The sheriff smiled.

Before anyone could say anything else, the deputy appeared in the doorway with a tray and a drink carrier. "Sheriff."

"What did you bring us, Dan?" the sheriff asked, stepping away from the door to allow the man to enter.

"Meatloaf sandwiches and chips with sweet tea." Dan sat the drink carrier on the table before settling the tray next to it. "John said we can return the tray later."

"Thanks, Dan." Jacob patted the deputy on the shoulder as the man went by, heading back out of the room. As soon as Dan was gone, the sheriff headed to the table and grabbed one of the sandwiches, a bag of chips, and a tea. "Help yourself, Agent Wayne."

"I never had a meatloaf sandwich before." Wayne grabbed some food and moved to a chair.

"John's meatloaf is very good." Sara too grabbed a sandwich.

Nick grabbed the autopsy file of the two women found here

and studied it as the other three ate in silence. Sara knew that vampires could eat normal food though they didn't get any nourishment from it, but they usually partake for the enjoyment of the taste. It also helped keep up the illusion that they were human.

Just as they finished their sandwiches and chips, Dan appeared again at the door. "We found Kirkland's car."

"Where?" Four voices rang out.

"Old Liam's gas station." The deputy said to the sheriff. "He said it was there when he opened this morning. Wes's keeping an eye on it."

"Good...I suppose you want to see it?" the sheriff asked Nick.

"Yes." Nick laid the file in his hand down and moved to the door.

Sara and Wayne followed just behind him with the sheriff. She doubted they would find anything at the gas station; the killer has been very methodical so far. He wouldn't have left anything behind of consequence.

"Becky, is Chris still at the dump site?" Jacob asked as they entered the lobby area.

"She was as of an hour ago."

"I'm going to need her. Can you get Alex to cover the dump site with Will?" The sheriff paused at the desk, and pulled out his phone. "We might have to call in a reserve or two."

"I'll take care of it, sheriff," Becky said.

"Good." The sheriff turned to the others. "I'll call Chris on the way. Just follow me."

"Alright." Nick agreed. "Let's go then."

The sheriff headed out the main door with the other three at his heels. He got into his car, and the others slid into the SUV, before following his car out of the parking lot.

CHAPTER FIVE

Sara was staring out the window, but she wasn't paying attention to the scenery while they drove. Working this case was interesting, and she had not been bored at all. She realized part of it was that she was being treated as an equal. There was no skepticism from Nick or Agent Wayne, and, of course, the sheriff knew she was telling the truth about her readings. After this case, she knew she could not go back to the clinic; ten years had indeed been enough.

"This gas station, is it used mainly by locals?" asked Wayne from the back seat, breaking into her thoughts. "It seems off the main highway."

"After they put in the new highway, some of the places along this road went out of business, but Liam's station became a hangout for the local teenagers and some weekend dragsters. Some of the farmers also use the station if they don't want to go to town proper."

"You seem to know a lot about this town," Wayne said. "I don't know this much about my hometown. Of course, I couldn't wait to leave while I was growing up."

"The donors at the clinic like to gossip," Sara said. Donors and clients alike talked to the blood handlers about everything while they waited through their turn. "Besides there's only a little over six thousand souls in this town, not like Logan where there's three hundred thousand."

Nick pulled into the gas station and parked behind the two sheriff's cars.

All three of them got out of the SUV and joined the sheriff next to his deputy. Kirkland's car was parked behind the station's building where it wouldn't be seen from the road. From where they were standing on the side lot, the silver car seemed undamaged and empty.

"Liam said he got here at six as usual and it was parked there. He didn't think anything of it since sometimes if something goes wrong, people leave their cars in his lot." Wes said. "However, no one came to claim it by noon so he came out and noticed there were no license plates. He waited until his afternoon person got here to call."

"He didn't see it last night when he came to close at ten?" the sheriff asked.

"No. I asked him when he finally left and he told me ten-thirty."

"So that gives us a time line of between ten-thirty and six," Nick said.

"I didn't see anything around the vehicle," the deputy said. "And the doors looked to be unlocked...I called Chris since Ron's still at the Inn."

"Chris said you did when I called her." Jacob said. "She should be here soon."

"You didn't see any blood?" Nick asked, his head tilted, obviously smelling something.

"Not near the car," Wes said. "There's a dark stain in the gravel just at the edge of the concrete slab."

"So a hundred feet away from the car?" Wayne asked since the slab went for at least a hundred feet past the car before it turned to gravel. "This must have been a meeting place."

"I wonder how they met in the first place." Jacob paused as another sheriff's car pulled in next to them. "There's Chris..."

The shapely red-head got out of the car, and Sara could see the drool gathering on Wayne's chin. Chris was rounded in all the right places, and kept herself in good shape which caused all the male deputies to fall all over themselves, even the married ones. The woman pulled a case from her trunk, and joined them, her green eyes gleaming. "You must be Agent Wayne," came her smoky voice. "I'm Deputy Chris Vaun, but you can call me Chris."

"Deputy Vaun, if you would check the stain at the end of the concrete first before you go to work on the car, I would appreciate it," Nick said. "I believe it is blood."

"Alright." She gave him an appreciative look, but remained professional and moved toward where the other deputy was pointing.

The others watched as she squatted and took a sample. She dug something out of her kit and did something they couldn't see. When Chris waved to them, they went over to her, leaving Wes by the cars.

Chris snapped a few pictures, then stood and looked at them. "It is indeed human blood and it's relatively fresh; last night sometime around midnight, if the test is right...I'm beta testing a new test that can pinpoint how long blood's been exposed to the air."

"So were all three of them here?" the sheriff asked. "There didn't seem to be any blood on the ground at the Inn."

"I'm going to check the car now," Chris said, heading that way as she spoke.

"The Sinq was here," Sara said. She had stepped off the concrete onto the gravel, and was listening to the whispers. There was a familiar feeling here. "This is where someone was killed as well."

"Just the two?" asked the sheriff.

"Only two people touched the gravel," Sara replied. "If someone else was on the concrete, I wouldn't get a read. The Sinq came upon another and the other died."

"Could you tell if the one was Vernon or Kirkland?" asked Nick.

"Well, it wasn't the man from the dump site so I don't think it was Kirkland. I haven't a reference for Vernon, but as we know for sure he's dead, I'd think it's him."

"DNA will tell us for sure." Jacob told them.

"If all three met here, there were at least two cars, maybe three." Wayne commented. "Kirkland's is the only one here. Perhaps we should find out if Vernon had a car and put a BOLO on it."

"I did that before I left the Inn," the sheriff told him. "Becky should have heard back from Logan by now and took care of it."

"Hopefully, the killer is still in possession of it," Nick said. "Or he was careless in disposing of it."

"So far he hasn't been careless with anything," the sheriff replied. "He definitely doesn't take chances."

"He does seem to plan everything out," Nick agreed.

"I don't think the last two were both planned," Sara said. "I think he planned one, but unexpected circumstances happened, and so two deaths. I don't know if he planned Kraig, but did the other woman for some reason, then had to go back to Kraig, or if he planned the other woman and found she was not what he wanted and had to do Kraig."

"You think this is his mistake, the one that will cause him to be caught," Nick said.

"Yes." Sara nodded. "I think he's unsettled about this, and probably second guessing himself. I would be."

"I agree," Nick told her. "I think Mr. Vernon is the reason for this 'mistake', and that's why he's dead."

"Vernon has to have something to do with one of the women," Wayne agreed.

"Yeah, he lied about one of them or something," the sheriff said. "I have a feeling there's going to be a lot of information to be found in Logan."

"We'll see tomorrow," Nick said as he turned to look toward the car. "I don't think this car was moved."

"They probably used Vernon's car for the dumping, then the killer's to get away," Wayne said. "But that would mean the other car is near here if they left with the body in Vernon's car, then came back for the killer's car."

"Unless the killer and Vernon came in the same car," Sara told him. Though she doubted that since the killer hadn't walked back from where he came from nor was there any sign of Kirkland walking back with the killer.

"There is that possibility," Nick agreed.

"There's an old barn near here." The sheriff gestured to the hill and trees behind them. "It's within walking distance."

"Is there a road to it?" asked Wayne.

"Not really." Jacob shook his head. "The house burned down

and the family moved away six years ago. Everything's overgrown, and the barn's about to fall over."

"So what do you call walking distance?" asked Wayne as he looked at the rise of ground and the scattering of trees.

"About a hundred yards on the other side of the hill, past a patch of trees." The sheriff smiled. "Anything under a mile is walking distance, Agent Wayne."

"It will be good exercise for you, Elliot." Nick laughed.

Wayne sighed and headed off toward where the sheriff was pointing.

"If he finds anything, we can take the cutoff from the road." The sheriff gestured towards the road. "It's just a few yards down, but it's rough."

"All right," Nick said. "It doesn't look like Deputy Vaun found anything inside the car."

"Maybe she'll find something in the trunk." Jacob turned and watched the female deputy go to the back of the car. "I think you're right that the car was left here while they used either Vernon's or the killer's to take the body to the Inn."

They all watched as the female deputy took pictures and examined the trunk.

Sara often wished she could read through concrete and asphalt; it would help her figure out what happened in many instances, and give the sheriff ideas he could follow up on. Although clues gotten from her were still iffy when it came to getting search warrants and things like that, the evidence found thanks to her was admissible in court and could still put people away. It was a fine line.

"I had Becky call Logan when I got to the office," the sheriff said as he unhooked his phone when it went off, and looked at the screen. "A Detective Olivia Yarnell is handling Kraig's case even though she's a missing person's detective since it started out as such. Becky says she'll be waiting for you at Vernon's apartment tomorrow morning. She said she'll have his information too since it seems related. Becky should have texted both you and your partner the address."

"I have my phone on vibrate, but I did feel it go off earlier."

"Becky also says she's got the photos." The sheriff tapped a few words, then hung his phone back on his belt. "Once Chris is done, the car will be towed to Benson's Garage and gone over by a mechanic to rule out mechanical problems. Wes'll keep an eye on it until then."

Nick's hand went to his phone, and he pulled it off his hip, his eyes going to the screen. "He hasn't looked inside the barn yet, but he's also found a flat area next to the barn where a car might have been parked."

"You want to head there now?" the sheriff asked. "Chris can join us when she's done."

"I am done." Chris said as she came up to them. "Registration says it's Kirkland's car, and guess what I found it the trunk...a .22 rifle.."

"So Kirkland was the shooter." The sheriff said. "I'll have Wes log it in at the station."

"Elliot says there's a car in the barn," Nick said as he tapped on his phone. "I'm telling him to wait for us."

"The Jackson farm?" Chris asked the sheriff.

"Yes, it's close so I figured the killer might have come from there."

"Good thing I brought extras for my kit," Chris said as she turned to head toward her car. "I'll see you there."

"Shall we go?" Jacob asked Nick. "Or did you need to look around here before we do?"

"We can go." Nick slipped his phone back on his hip and moved toward the cars. "I think the barn will be more enlightening than here."

Sara and the sheriff followed him to the cars. The sheriff got into his car while Sara slid into the passenger seat of the SUV. Nick stood for a moment with the driver's door open and looked around before sliding into the SUV.

"What is it?" Sara asked.

"I don't know." Nick shook his head, and started the vehicle. He pulled out and followed the sheriff's car as it moved slowly down the road and then suddenly turned into an overgrown area. "I don't see a road."

"There isn't really. The Jackson family just brush hogged a lane from the road to their farm and kept it mowed. They were self-sufficient, and only came to town once a week." Sara gripped the hand hold above the door as the going got rougher. "When the house burned down, the family sold the animals, put the land up for sale, and moved to Logan."

Nick pulled up beside the sheriff's car in a large overgrown area with what was left of a burnt two story house on one side and a leaning barn and corral on the other. He and Sara both slid out of the SUV and joined the sheriff in front of the vehicles.

Sara had immediately been assaulted by whispers when she touched the ground. She knew that Kirkland and the Sinq had been here, and had left in another car, both alive, but she kept silent for the moment.

"I took a few pictures," Wayne said as he stepped out of the barn and moved toward them. "The building's really unstable."

Another sheriff's car pulled up and Chris got out. She pulled her case from the back seat and moved to join them. "I'll dust the trunk for prints, but then I think we should move the car out of the barn before I examine it completely."

"Part of the building is resting on the car," Wayne said. "The trunk and the back doors are clear, but the front part of the car is holding up the back roof."

"All right. I guess I'll just have to be careful." Chris moved to the barn and disappeared inside.

"This happened six years ago?" Nick asked, gesturing toward the burnt skeleton of a farmhouse.

"Yes," the sheriff replied. "I see where you're going with this, but it was in all the papers here and in Logan so anyone here at the time, living or vacationing, would know about the house burning."

"Things seem to be leading us to Logan," Nick said. "Tomorrow should be enlightening as well."

The sheriff's phone went off and he pulled it off his belt, looking at the screen. "Becky says she's got a pix of Vernon's car, and she's sending it now."

Wayne's phone went off and he looked at it. "That's the car in the barn."

"Did you find anything in the barn itself?" Nick asked.

"There are two distinct set of footprints in the debris on the floor," Wayne answered. "So there definitely were two people. There were some strange marks along side one set of footprints as if something dragged the debris."

"You got close ups of the footprints?" Nick's tone really

didn't make it a question.

"Close enough to tell that one is size 11, and the other size 12," Wayne said. "I didn't see anything else of importance in the barn, but a car was parked next to the barn. I found a tire impression and snapped a picture."

"I'll have Chris do a plaster impression as well," the sheriff said. "When we get back, you can show the picture to Dan, and maybe he can tell you which car it came off of. His family runs the main tire shop, and Dan worked there growing up."

"I'll do that," Wayne agreed.

"Sara, you've been awfully quiet," the sheriff said, looking at her.

"This is where the Sinq came from, and walked to the station. Kirkland and the Sinq weren't here long when they came here." Sara paused. "I can do a deep reading if you want but I doubt there's much more than what we already know."

"I agree." Nick said. "I think this was just another dump site."

"Chris says she didn't find anything in the back seat; no blood or hair." The sheriff said, looking at his phone. "There were some receipts in the area between the front seats, and the registration says it's Vernon's car, but there's nothing of importance in the glove box, just insurance papers."

"She's headed for the trunk then, I presume." Nick said.

"Dusting it now, she texted." The sheriff replied. "She's left the imager and scanner in her car so she'll have to send the prints when she comes out."

"For a rural county you sure have expensive toys," Wayne commented.

"Half of those living in this town are vampires, Agent Wayne," the sheriff told him. "Including most of the advisors of the town council as well as a few of the council members. Of course that's not common knowledge. I need something; the council finds the funds one way or another. Half of my equipment was paid for from personal funds of some of the council members or their aides."

Wayne looked at Sara who laughed. "I'm not a vampire. I just work for them."

"There's blood in the trunk," the sheriff said, looking at his phone. "Human blood…So all three of them were at the gas station during one point, and they did use Vernon's car to transport the body to the Inn."

"I wonder why the killer didn't kill Kirkland and leave the body here," Wayne said. "Kirkland's a liability after all."

"Maybe he has something to do with the killer's 'unfinished business'," the sheriff said. "The killer was in Logan this morning to drop off the envelope at the reporter's."

"Maybe they're working together now," Wayne speculated.

"I don't think so," Sara said. "Kirkland was very angry, both at the Inn and here."

"You think he is angry at the killer," Nick said, "and is being coerced."

"Yes." Sara nodded. "I think the killer is keeping him from doing something."

"Maybe keeping him from stalking you," Nick told her. "If Kirkland is the man who shot at you."

"Maybe." Sara shrugged.

"Becky says that Ron is done at the Inn," the sheriff said. "I told her to tell him to come here and pick up the evidence that Chris will have for him. I think we should go back to the office and look at those photos Agent Wayne took at the Inn as well as the ones he took here."

"I agree," Nick said. "We can't do anything more until we get the various reports back."

"Wes's done at the gas station." The sheriff paused. "This car's not going anywhere so I'll have night shift and day shift do a few checks until I figure out what to do with it."

"Just drag it out," Wayne said. "I doubt it matters what happens to the barn."

"I probably will." The sheriff tapped on his phone for a minute, then slipped it back on his belt. "I'll meet you back at the office."

The other three nodded and moved from the front of the vehicles, sliding into the SUV. Nick turned the vehicle around and followed their tracks back out to the road, heading toward the town proper.

CHAPTER SIX

"I hope there's a new pot of coffee waiting," Wayne commented into the waiting silence. "I could use another dose of caffeine."

"I'm sure Becky put another pot on when the sheriff texted her back." Sara smiled.

"I know the Bureau had people intercepting cell calls, but with the new tech services, it's harder to intercept them. However, most law enforcement still use the old radio system," Nick commented. "I noticed that the sheriff and his people for the most part text as well, using the radio only a few times. I know why the Bureau uses only secured lines and texts, but why here?"

"A lot of the residents of Kester county have scanners," Sara told him. "And the sheriff has had reporters show up and mess up crime scenes. Therefore all the deputies are on a secure network like the FBI, and only use the radio if they want everyone to hear the broadcast."

"That still doesn't explain why texting and not calling," Wayne said.

"The ringing could come at an inconvenient time, like the middle of a stand-off, but the vibration of a text doesn't cause a problem." Sara shrugged. "The sheriff's always texted."

Nick pulled into a parking spot in front of the sheriff's office, and shut off the vehicle. All three of them got out of the SUV, and headed into the building.

"Along with the address I sent to you for John Vernon, I got that he's a thirty-year-old delivery driver for Nash Delivery where he's worked for the past six years," Becky said by way of greeting. "He's had two drunk and disorderlies three years ago, but nothing since. Detective Yarnell will probably have more information tomorrow for you."

"Thank you," Nick said. "Do you have the pictures?"

"Right here." Becky handed over the file containing the pictures. "Do you have anymore to process? I can get Dan to do them right away."

Wayne slipped off the camera from around his neck, and took the memory card out handing it to Becky. "There's only ten photos on the card. Shouldn't take him long."

Dan came out of a door from the other hallway and moved to the desk. Becky handed him the memory card, and he went back down the hallway to the room he had come out of.

"I made a new pot of both the coffee and the tea," Becky told them. "John came back for the tray and left some cookies by the pots."

"Excellent," Wayne said, rubbing his hands together.

Nick rolled his eyes, then gestured towards the conference room with his free hand. "Let's get started on these photos."

The humans headed towards the conference room with Nick following behind them. As soon as they entered, Wayne made a beeline for the coffee pot and cookies, while Sara and Nick headed for the table.

"Are we going to divide and conquer?" Sara asked as they all sat down. "Each of us take some photos and go through them?"

"That will probably be the quickest way." Nick set the file between them and opened it, grabbing a few of the photos. "You said you think that scene at the Inn was for us. There has to be something in these photos then."

"The killer definitely wanted us to know that Vernon was a liar." Sara flipped through some pictures. "He took the body to the Inn. He wanted to say something."

"Maybe he just wanted to bring attention to Kirkland," Wayne said.

"I think that was part of it," Nick said. "But I also think Sara's right that he wanted to say something else."

"There was nothing in that room." Wayne laid down the photos in his hands. "It was as if it had not been used, except for the closet. There was clothing and a suitcase inside."

"Then maybe it was the body," Sara said.

Wayne looked through the photos, and laid out eight photos on the table. "He wasn't holding anything."

Sara looked over the photos, then tapped one. "Notice the slashes on the T-shirt. The inverted triangle with the line across the lower quarter."

"A symbol?" Wayne asked.

"It's an elemental symbol," Sara told them. "One of four."

"Earth, air, water, fire," Nick said.

"Yes." Sara nodded. "He knew I'd recognize it once I looked past the blood."

"Recognize what?" the sheriff asked as he entered the room.

"The symbol the killer slashed in the T-shirt," Sara replied as she picked up the picture. She handed the picture to the sheriff who immediately looked at it. "It's the symbol for Earth."

"He mentioned a mission in his note," Nick said. "And he seems to know about your gift. Do you think he's someone you worked with before?"

"It isn't any of the sheriff's deputies," Sara told him. "But among the Staties or the Logan PD? I don't know. None of the ones who worked with me at the scenes were Sinqs though."

"You said the locals know you consult for the sheriff, but don't know how." Wayne said. "But that the gossipers say you're psychic. You sure the deputies haven't told anyone?"

"The deputies are the ones who passed around that I'm psychic," Sara replied.

"To quiet the gossipers, no doubt," Nick said.

"Correct," Sara nodded. "The gossipers can be outrageous with their stories if not curbed."

"And persistent," the sheriff added.

"Logan keeps coming up in this case," Nick commented. "I'm inclined to believe the killer lives there but has local ties."

"Could be. Many locals have ties to Logan," the sheriff said. He laid a file on the table, and tapped it. "These are the photos you gave Dan earlier. He said the tread pattern in the impressions look to be from tires of an older model car. His father told him they discontinued those tires six years ago so tires were either on the car that long or they were bought at a used tire shop. Dan said his father doesn't carry them. Becky's having Dan call the used tire shops in Logan."

"If we get a suspect that may help." Nick paused as he opened the new file. "Did you find out anything more at the barn?"

"Just that Chris is sure the car was the transport for the body. She found hairs, more blood, and some fibers." The sheriff pulled out two memory cards from his shirt pocket, and handed them to Wayne. "Dan told me he transferred all the pictures to the computer system so you can use these again."

"I'll transfer them to my laptop before I do that," Wayne said. "But thanks."

"There's not much detail in these footprints," Nick said as he looked at a picture from the new file. "Can't tell if they're boots or shoes, nor is there any tread pattern."

"The police lab won't be able to tell what shoe or boot they came from," Wayne agreed. "But at least we have the size. There's also the marks in the debris around the one set of footprints, almost as if something stirred the rubbish up."

"It does look like marks made in debris by something being dragged or as if someone used a broom ," Nick agreed. "But if they took the trouble with a broom, the footprints would be completely gone."

"I've seen similar markings before," the sheriff said when he looked at one of the photos. "From a woman's long dress dragging the ground. But that doesn't make sense."

"I didn't see a third set of footprints but is there a third person involved in this somehow?" Wayne asked. "Or perhaps the killer was dragging something."

"Only the Sinq and Kirkland were at the barn," Sara said. "Of that I'm sure. No other energy was there."

"What if the killer's accomplice is a Sinq too?" Wayne asked.

"Sinqs are rare," Sara told him. "There is also what you would call an after taste to the blankness. The Sinq at the barn was the same one at the Inn."

"I wonder what the killer did with Kirkland after they left the barn," Wayne said. "The killer can't drag Kirkland around with him everywhere."

"The Sinq has a purpose for Kirkland, I think," Sara said. "Or he would have killed him already."

"He might have," Wayne told her. "We don't know where either of them is right now."

"I'd use him as a fall guy," the sheriff said. "Keep him on ice until I needed him."

Kirkland would indeed be the perfect fall guy, Sara agreed. All the circumstantial evidence pointed to him. A body was found in his cabin and his car was at the primary crime scene. Also there's the cigarette butts near the dump site, showing he was there if the DNA came back as his.

"If we didn't have Sara, we'd believe the killer was Kirkland." The sheriff said. "All we'd need is Kirkland to show up as an apparent suicide."

"Or have a dramatic shootout, ending in his death," Wayne added.

"Either way we'd say 'case closed'," The sheriff said. "And not look any further."

"And he'd find a new dump site," Nick said. "Maybe even move."

"Like he did before." Sara paused. "The files said the body and skeletons in Wyoming were found two years ago, then the mummified remains were found last summer."

"Yeah, an agent went for a training seminar, and it was the talk of the conference about the mummies found a couple of months before," Wayne said. "So the killer had to have moved or took vacation in those two states. The Nevada M.E. said the remains had been there for a long time; at least a decade, he reckoned, but he couldn't tell for sure passed that."

"Maybe he has a job that requires travel," the sheriff said. "He could be assigned a district, and then reassigned."

"We've looked at a few major sales companies in the areas, but none have panned out so far," Wayne replied. "However, there are literally thousands of companies that require travel, and we have little to go on."

"I think we've done as much as we can for today." Nick put the pictures back into their files and set them aside. "We're going to be leaving early in the morning for Logan."

"I think you're right. We should call it an evening," Wayne agreed.

"I don't feel like cooking so the café is the next destination," Sara said.

"I agree with that," Wayne said as they all stood. "I could go for more 'home' cooking."

"John actually does make everything from scratch," the sheriff told him.

"All the more reason to eat there," Wayne replied as he led the way out of the room. "Nick only likes to eat snooty food."

"I have refined taste," Nick said.

"Whatever." Wayne snorted.

"John was a big city chef before he came here," the sheriff said. "So if you ask real nice he might make you something, Agent Issaro."

"I'll remember that." Nick paused as he motioned Sara and Wayne towards the door. "Shall we go?"

"Of course," they both said together, and went out the door.

"We're driving there." Nick slipped past them, and opened the driver door to the SUV. "I don't feel like walking."

Sara and Wayne slid into the SUV without a word, and Nick drove them the three blocks to the brick-faced café. Entering the building, they could see it had a counter and several booths along the walls with a few tables in the center. Several people were sitting on the stools at the counter, and two of the booths were occupied.

Sara led them all to one of the booths with a window, motioning Wayne to slide in first.

"Why do I have to be the one in the back?" Wayne complained.

"I ain't sitting in the back, and I doubt Nick will," Sara told him.

"Nick's paying, that's all I'm saying," Wayne said as he slid into the booth.

"I agree," Sara said as she sat beside him. She looked at Nick who was sitting across from her. "You sure you don't want to go to the clinic?"

"I am fine." He paused as the waitress handed them menus. "I will tell you should that change though."

"Alright," Sara conceded. "What's the special tonight, Jane?"

"Same as lunch." The waitress laughed. "John's on a meatloaf kick today."

"Well, I enjoyed lunch so I'll have the special." Sara handed back the menu as she spoke. "And ice tea to drink."

"I'll have the same," Wayne said.

"Nothing for me, thank you."

"Alright, I'll be back with the meals soon." The waitress grabbed the other menus and left for the counter.

"You said you were just getting used to this gift when you moved here," Wayne said as he relaxed against the wall. "How did you acquire it?"

Sara waited until the waitress left after giving them their drinks before looking at Wayne. "A dying man passed it on to me."

"A shaman?" Nick asked.

"He carried that title. He wasn't a true shaman though since he didn't have all four elements." Sara took a sip of her tea. "There are very few true shaman any more. The stress of being a true shaman is something very few can handle."

"I can imagine," Nick said. "The voices in one's head all the time."

"As I said it can drive one insane, homicidally so." Sara paused as the waitress set their food before them. "Compartmentalization is key."

"Why you?" Wayne asked. "I mean, didn't he have an apprentice?"

"It was his 'apprentice' who poisoned him," Sara told him. "He tried to kill me as well."

"He was that desperate to be a shaman?" Wayne asked.

"He was that desperate for the respect and power that comes along with being a shaman." Sara sighed. "Shaman are powerful people in certain societies, and he thought he could command respect--and money--from others if he took the title."

"You have to earn respect, though certain titles do bestow a certain amount on their bearers," Nick said. "But to keep it, you have to deserve it."

"I don't think he realized that." Sara shook her head. "He thought only of the power."

"What happened to this 'apprentice'?" Wayne asked.

"He's dead." Sara paused as she pushed her empty plate away. "There are some things you shouldn't mess with."

Both Nick and Wayne looked at her when she said that.

"You know you shouldn't piss off Mother Nature," Sara told them.

"So the earth is feminine?" Nick asked.

"It nurtures us so it has what we call feminine qualities." Sara took a sip of her tea before continuing. "Each element has both masculine and feminine qualities, but each also has more of one or the other. Fire is more masculine, the earth more feminine while air is more masculine, and water more feminine."

"How do you know all of this?" Nick asked. "If both the shaman and his apprentice died, who gave you this information?"

"Remember I told you I knew a Native American woman who heard the wind?" Sara paused and waited for Nick's nod. "She spoke to me. I didn't believe her at first, of course. Who would?"

"I suppose it was similar to when we revealed ourselves," Nick said. "Much disbelief and…misunderstandings."

"Yes." Sara nodded. That was an understatement on both counts.. "Not the best of times."

"How are the pies here?" Wayne asked as he pushed his empty plate away. "I saw yesterday that they have cherry."

"As the sheriff said, John makes everything from scratch, including the pies." Sara waved the waitress over. "Agent Wayne would like to try John's cherry pie, Jane."

"One slice coming up," the waitress said as she turned towards the counter.

"She's John's companion?" Nick asked in a low voice when the waitress was out of hearing range. "A vampire's scent is all over her."

"I never asked, but they live together," Sara replied. "And he stopped coming to the clinic."

"He cooks pretty good for a vampire," Wayne commented with a grin.

"I only burned the food that one time, Elliot," Nick said with a sigh.

"Once is all it takes," Wayne said.

"Agent Wayne ain't your companion, is he?" Sara asked. After all, that would explain their ease with each other if they had been.

"Hell, no," Wayne said. "I like women."

"Besides he's too high maintenance," Nick added which made Wayne sputter.

"So I see." Sara laughed.

The waitress returned and set a plate in front of Wayne with a large slice of pie and whipped cream. She laid the receipt on the table as well before heading back to the counter.

"I think it's time we head for your apartment," Nick said. "Elliot, bring me another change in the morning, and we'll leave once I'm ready."

"Alright." Wayne nodded. "I'll see you in the morning then."

Both Sara and Nick slid out of the booth and Nick headed toward the cash register at the counter while Sara moved toward the door. By the time she made her way to the door though, Nick came up behind her and opened it for her. Once outside, Nick and Sara headed to the SUV. Both ready to call it a night.

CHAPTER SEVEN

LOGAN
POPULATION: 234,134

Sara glanced at the sign, and then turned her attention forward. They had made the three hour drive in two hours and fifteen minutes with Nick driving.

Last night, she had gone straight to her room when Nick and she arrived at her apartment. She spent part of the night on her laptop, but most of the night going over what they had learned that day. Sleep had over taken her as she was going over the facts for the third time.

"David just texted about Mayer's visitor log." Wayne looked at his phone. "He said Kirkland visited Mayer every week. David faxed a hard copy of the last three months' logs to the sheriff's office for us to look over later."

"Good," Nick said. "What about who claimed the body?"

"It wasn't claimed. It was buried by the state."

"Mmmm. Did he get more info on Kirkland?"

Wayne tapped his phone. "All he found was the assault charge criminally. He faxed the basics to the sheriff's office."

"What about this Detective Yarnell?" Nick asked. "Did you have David look her up?"

"Becky texted you Yarnell's file," Wayne replied.

"All that said was that she's been a detective for three years, the last two in missing persons," Nick replied. "And that she's worked on a couple cases that turned into homicides this last year. David knows what we need."

"Yarnell's file is thin," Wayne told him. "She was brought up on sexual harassment charges two times in the last year though."

"She didn't file them?" Nick asked.

"No, they were filed against her, and from what was implied they were swept under the rug because of her father." Wayne shook his head. "He's friends with the police commissioner."

Nick was silent for a moment, then asked, "Anything else?"

"From what David found she doesn't take 'no' for an answer," Wayne said.

"We'll see," Nick told him. "We're almost there."

Sara glanced out at the building-lined street and spotted a woman standing on the stoop of one ahead. "I think that's the one."

"It is." Nick pulled into a parking spot behind a tan sedan. "That must be Detective Yarnell."

The woman had long dark hair in a bun and wore skin-tight jeans and T-shirt. She was shapely with a cuteness about her face. Her badge was hooked on her belt next to her weapon, and she was holding a file.

They got out of the SUV and moved toward the woman. Sara noticed the look in the woman's eyes when she looked at Nick, and silently sighed. The woman was lusting after the handsome vampire.

"I'm Detective Yarnell," the woman said to Nick with a smile, ignoring Wayne who was closer. "You can call me Olivia."

"I'm Agent Issaro," Nick said. "My partner Agent Wayne, and Consultant Phillips."

"A pleasure," Yarnell said, her eyes never leaving Nick. "Why don't your partner and consultant go in, and I'll bring you up to date?"

"Why don't you just bring us all up to date," Nick said, his voice bland.

Yarnell blinked, then handed the file to Wayne. "CSU was here yesterday."

"When your Crime Scene Unit is finished with their report,

make sure to send a copy to both us and the Kester County sheriff," Nick commented.

"And the DNA results came in this morning. The one body is Kraig's so CSU is at her apartment right now and should be finished soon." Yarnell paused. "Vernon had a live-in girlfriend, a Misty Wells, who we haven't been able to find. My partner thinks the other body might be hers since she's not been seen for over a week."

"Could be," Wayne said as he flipped through the file. "These preliminary reports say that there's no blood or struggle evident in the apartment."

"But there are packing boxes in the bedroom and living room," Yarnell said.

"So one or the other was moving or both were," Wayne said.

"Agent Issaro, why don't you and I go to Kraig's apartment while Agent Wayne and Ms. Phillips look Vernon's apartment over?" Yarnell asked with another smile.

Sara could almost feel the lust coming off the woman. Of course, she couldn't blame her; Nick was very handsome. However, the woman didn't seem to notice that Nick wasn't interested, either that or she didn't care.

"Elliot, did you want to go with Detective Yarnell and look over Kraig's apartment while Sara and I stay here?" Nick asked.

Wayne's eyes flickered over Yarnell, then went to Nick. "Not really. We can all go later if you decide we should."

Sara hid her smile as Yarnell frowned. She wondered if Yarnell caught the underlining meaning or just didn't like that Nick had asked Wayne to go with her.

"Is the apartment locked and sealed?" Nick asked.

"It's locked, but we didn't think it had to be sealed," Yarnell told him. "There's an officer with a key waiting at the door."

"Excellent." Nick put a hand on Sara's back and guided her toward the door. "We will contact you later if we need anything else."

It was a clear dismissal but Yarnell stood there for a moment longer before heading down the stoop toward her car while Wayne followed Nick and Sara inside. The lobby was similar to Sara's, and the three of them headed up the stairs with barely a glance around them.

"She's probably going to be at Kraig's apartment when we get there," Wayne commented. "She won't give up easily."

"Probably." Nick paused as he continued up another flight. "Fourth floor, right?"

"Yes. What is with all these walk-ups?" Wayne shook his head from behind Sara.

"Cheaper to build and cheaper to insure," Sara told them. "Or so I was told by my landlord."

Nick stepped out into the fourth floor hallway and headed toward the uniformed man standing by one of the doors. He stopped in front of the officer and pulled out his wallet, showing his credentials. "This is my partner Agent Wayne and Consultant Phillips."

"Detective Yarnell said you'd be by," the officer said as he unlocked the door and pushed it open. "I'll lock up as soon as you're done."

"Thank you," Nick said as he followed Sara and Wayne inside.

There was a small kitchenette to the left and a bathroom to the right. Past them there was a small living area which had a door to the left; the bedroom, no doubt.

"Kraig's initial missing person's report is in here," Wayne said, his face in the file he carried. "Vernon's not mentioned in it so he wasn't a friend."

"What about his girlfriend?" asked Nick.

"I don't see her name in the list of friends either." Wayne closed the file and pulled out his phone. "I'll have David look up the girlfriend."

"Her last name is Wells. I wonder if she's related to David," Nick said.

"That would be weird," Wayne said as he tapped his phone. "How do you want to handle this?"

"The initial report says there's no sign of intruders?" asked Nick.

"No forced entry," Wayne told him.

"We knew he met the killer at the gas station," Sara said. "Did he report his girlfriend missing?"

"The report doesn't say." Wayne tapped his phone some more. "I'm texting Detective Yarnell to see.".

"Did CSU find a daily planner or calendar, I wonder," Nick commented. "He had to have come in contact with the killer somehow."

"And lied to him," Sara added as she wandered into the kitchen. "I have a drawer in my kitchen where I keep correspondence and a planner."

"The planner will probably be gone if there was one," Wayne said. "Yarnell said it was a work colleague who reported her missing just yesterday."

Sara pulled open a top drawer and said, "Bingo."

"Correspondence?" asked Nick.

"Yep." Sara flipped through the envelopes. "Some bills and a couple of letters from a Catholic church addressed to Vernon. Nothing with Wells' name on it."

Wayne joined her in the kitchen and took one of the envelopes from the Catholic church. "This is the same church Kraig went to, according to the missing persons' report."

"Then perhaps we should go there before going to Kraig's apartment," Nick said.

"Yarnell will still be there, you know," Wayne said with a wink toward Sara..

Nick moved to where he could give Wayne a glare.

Raising his hands, Wayne said, "Alright. Sorry."

Sara had taken the letter out of the other envelope and was skimming it. "This is thanking Vernon for volunteering at a charity function. It is signed by the secretary of a Father Clarke."

"This one is signed by a Father Martin," Wayne said as he scanned the one he held. "It's also for him volunteering at a charity function."

"Text Yarnell and see how long she thinks CSU will be." Nick looked at Wayne. "I'd like the initial report of Kraig's apartment when we get there after talking to the priests."

"Right." Wayne pulled his phone out again after handing the letter to Sara. "You think the killer met them through a church function?"

"That's my theory," Nick said. "You would trust someone you met that way."

"I agree," Sara said. "The other victims weren't very social but they all were active in their churches."

"Yarnell thinks less than two hours." Wayne took the two letters from Sara and slipped them into the file under his arm. "We can get a list from the priests of who volunteered at these functions, and I'll text Wyoming and Nevada to get lists of church volunteers."

"Good." Nick headed out of the kitchen and moved toward the front door. "Let's go."

"You sure you don't want us to look around some more?" Wayne asked as he and Sara followed Nick. "We might find something else."

"I want to get that list of volunteers and talk to the priests," Nick said as he opened the door. He allowed the other two to exit, then closed the door behind him. "Officer, we're done for now. Thank you."

"I'm to head back to the station," the officer said. "But the Super will let you in if you need to come back."

"Alright," Wayne said. "Thanks."

The three of them left the officer at the door and headed down the stairs.

"David says the girlfriend's not related," Wayne said as he looked at his phone. "She was born in Heasley, Wyoming."

"That's interesting." Nick paused. "I wonder if she knew any of the victims from there."

"She could have since she worked as a secretary at the same Catholic church that one of the victims went to," Wayne said. "David will get the volunteer lists from the churches in Wyoming and Nevada."

"Excellent," Nick said as he stepped into the lobby after the other two. "She worked at the church here?"

"No," Wayne said as he opened the lobby door, allowing the others to pass him. "But she did work for a charity."

They headed down the stoop and got into the SUV.

"Which street?" Nick asked as he started the vehicle.

"Risen," Wayne told him. "It's off Spring Street."

"Ironic name," Nick said as he pulled into the street. "A church on Risen."

"Did you spend last night studying a map of Logan on your phone?" Sara asked.

"Just a few hours," Nick replied.

"He always does that," Wayne said. "He likes to drive, and he hates asking directions."

"Waste of time," Nick said as he turned onto Spring Street.

"David says the charity Wells worked for, Lander Charity For the Blind, was one closely aligned with St. Michaels," Wayne said, looking at his phone again. "Father John Martin is the liaison for all the charities there."

"Did David get anything on him yet?" Nick asked.

"John Martin is assistant Pastor of St. Michaels with Father Marcus Clarke as the Pastor. There are two other priests at the church; a Father Aaron Travis and a Father James Christopher. David hasn't run a search on any of them yet."

"Father Martin would probably be the one to talk to," Sara said. "Since he's the liaison for the charities."

"I agree," Nick said as he pulled into a parking slot near the tall gothic-looking church. "He would have knowledge of the volunteers."

The three of them got out of the SUV and headed toward the church. Nick opened the door then followed the others inside.

Inside was a typical Catholic church; pews to the left and right with an aisle leading up to the raised alter and podiums. There was a choir loft and then along the sides there were confessionals. Statues of the blessed Mary and Saints were scattered about as well.

Two men were standing just before the raised alter at the separating railing. One was in a black suit, and the other was dressed in black pants and a black shirt with the white collar of a priest. The priest was in his thirties with blond hair while the other man was older with graying black hair. They were in some kind of discussion with the older man gesturing when he spoke.

Nick, Wayne, and Sara headed that way, and paused a few feet away from the two men. Both men turned toward the three newcomers as the two became aware of them.

"May I help you?" the priest asked.

"I'm Agent Issaro, this is my partner Agent Wayne, and Consultant Phillips. We'd like to talk to Father Martin if we could."

"I'm Father Martin," the priest said. "What is this about?"

"I'm sure the police have talked to you about Ms. Kraig,"

Nick said. "But we'd also like to talk to you about Misty Wells and John Vernon."

"Excuse me, I'm Arthur Hoss," the man in the suit said. "Ms. Wells worked for me."

"I'm sure the police will speak to you soon, Mr. Hoss," Nick said. "Once they are sure of the facts in this case."

"We were wondering, Father Martin, if we could have a list of your volunteers," Wayne said. "We understand that Mr. Vernon volunteered frequently at your charity functions."

"He and Misty both did," Father Martin said. "I will have to get Father Clarke's approval."

"My approval for what, John?" came a voice from the left.

Everyone turned toward the sound to see an elderly priest standing there. He must have come from one of the confessionals, Sara thought. His hair was solid white from age and he wore the same black clothes as Father Martin with the white collar. Faded blue eyes squinted at them as he moved closer. He had to be at least sixty, but he still moved with ease.

"The agents want a list of our volunteers," Father Martin said.

"Is this about Mr. Vernon?" Father Clarke asked Nick. When Nick nodded, Clarke sighed. "He was a troubled young man."

"How so?" Wayne asked.

"I'm sure you know I can't tell you what we talked about in confessional," Clarke said. "But as I said he was a troubled young man...I see no reason why they cannot have the list, John."

"As you wish," said Father Martin as he headed towards the door in the wall behind Father Clarke. "I will have Ruth make a copy then. I'll be right back."

"Did Misty Wells work for you personally, Mr. Hoss?" asked Wayne.

"Yes," Hoss said. "I'm the head of Lander's P.R. department, and she was one of my assistants. There are two other assistants."

"Was she assigned certain duties?" Wayne questioned.

"She mainly coordinated with the press about what Lander's does." Hoss told him. "A lot of the press set-ups were her doing."

Father Martin came up to them and handed Wayne two sheets of paper. "Ruth had a copy already made up."

"Thank you, Father," Wayne said as he glanced at the pages. "I'll look these over later."

"Thank you, Gentlemen, for your time," Nick said as he took a step away from the three men. "We'll let you get back to your discussion with Mr. Hoss, Father Martin."

"Yes, and thanks again for the list," Wayne added as he turned down the aisle.

Nick put his hand on Sara's back and escorted her toward the front doors while Wayne followed behind them. They went out the doors and down the stairs, heading toward their vehicle. The three of them kept silent until they were back in the SUV.

"I smelled a scent from the cabin in there," Nick said. "but with all the other odors present I couldn't pin-point where the smell was from."

"Do you think one of them is the killer?" Wayne asked.

"I don't know." Nick shook his head. "Sara?"

"I don't know either." Sara looked toward the church. "No earth, no read."

"So you couldn't tell if one of them was the Sinq?" Wayne asked.

"Not unless he touches me," Sara told him. "Or I touch him."

"That's not happening," Nick said as he started the vehicle.

"So the killer could still be one of the volunteers listed on these pages?" Wayne asked.

"All I know is that I smelled the same scent in the church that was at the cabin," Nick told him as he pulled out into the street. "Have David run a check on the volunteers, and include the three men we just met."

"Right." Wayne snapped pictures of the pages and tapped a bit on his phone. "David can compare this list to the others and see if any correlate."

"We'll get the initial report of Kraig's apartment, have a brief look around, then head back to Debow," Nick said as he navigated the vehicle towards Kraig's apartment. "Hopefully, by the time we're there, David will have something for us."

"Yarnell says we might want to wait on Kraig's apartment," Wayne said, looking at his phone. "She says we might be interested more in what was called in half an hour ago."

"Oh?" Nick glanced at Wayne in the rear view mirror, noting the seriousness of his voice.

Wayne raised his eyes from his phone. "A mutilated body was

found in an apartment on Croster Street."

CHAPTER EIGHT

Nick pulled in behind a police cruiser and turned off the SUV. All three of them got out of the vehicle and stood for a moment looking at the apartment building. On the outside it looked similar to Vernon's walk-up, except there were police personnel standing all around and going in and out the front door.

"Agent Issaro," called Yarnell as she stepped out the front door onto the stoop.

The two agents and Sara moved to join her there.

"You said there's a mutilated body?" Wayne spoke as soon as they were close enough to be heard without shouting. "Similar to the ones in Debow?"

"When the assistant M.E. arrived, he noticed the similarity to your case and called me." Yarnell paused. "Agent Wayne and your consultant can go in while we discuss this, if you want."

"Just give us a rundown now," Nick said. "And then we'll all go in."

"Doctor Helen Myers, 45," Yarnell began. "She didn't show up for work at her clinic this morning so one of her assistants came over here first break she had, found the door open, and went in. The body was found on the bed, but the womb was on the night stand."

"Are you going to handle this case or is it going to be assigned to another detective?" Wayne asked.

"The homicide detectives are inside, but I'll be working with them," Yarnell said. "We're now officially a task force working with the sheriff's department and you."

"What's the clinic's name?" Wayne asked as he pulled out his phone. "And what did she do there?"

"Kester County Women's Clinic," Yarnell said. "And she was the head doctor. I think I should mention that the clinic was notorious for performing a lot of abortions."

"Are there any other clinics with that reputation?" asked Sara before either agent could say anything about this tidbit.

"No." Yarnell shook her head. "If you want an abortion you came to KCWC. The other clinics, some of which are privately run, have good reps."

"Are there other female doctors?" Sara continued to question. "at KCWC?"

"I see where this is going," Yarnell said, pulling out her own phone. She hit speed dial and put it to her ear. "Max, we need protection details on the other doctors of KCWC. The killer might go after them as well."

"You think this is his 'unfinished business'?" asked Wayne.

"I'm not sure." Sara shook her head. "I believe the other victims all had abortions or got rid of their babies somehow."

"That's why you wanted their medical records," Nick said.

"Yes." Sara paused. "However, we know Kirkland is a red herring, but that doesn't mean there can't be more."

"Meaning he might have killed the doctor to get us looking in the wrong direction," Nick said.

"Anti-abortion protesters who have threatened the doctor, for example," Wayne agreed.

"It's something to keep in mind," Sara said.

"Noted," Nick said. "Detective Yarnell, Dr. Myers wasn't a practicing Catholic, was she?"

Yarnell slipped her phone back on her hip, then raised her eyes to Nick. "I don't know. My partner's taking care of the other doctors."

"Excellent." Nick laid his hand on Sara's back and guided her through the open front door into the lobby. He continued to guide her along to the apartment the police officers were guarding and where overall-covered CSU personnel were coming in and out.

"I'm overjoyed that we're part of a task force," Wayne said, coming up behind them. "Aren't you?"

Nick threw him a look over his shoulder, then asked the officer standing on the right side of the door, "Where's the homicide detectives?"

"Still in the bedroom."

"Thank you." Nick guided Sara inside with Wayne a step behind.

The apartment was laid out more like Sara's than Vernon's with the kitchen and living room almost one big area and two doors on the right. Everything was shiny and glittery. You could tell a person of means lived here.

The three of them headed toward the open bedroom door where two men were standing just inside. One was balding and going on fifty, the other had a full head of black hair and was in his thirties. Both wore cheap black suits and even cheaper watches.

"Detectives, I'm Agent Issaro. This is my partner Agent Wayne, and consultant Sara Phillips."

"I'm Ragland," the older detective said. "And this is my partner Roth."

"So what do we have?" Nick asked as he stepped further into the room.

"As you can see it's not a pretty picture," Ragland said as he gestured toward the bed.

A middle aged woman with blond hair in what was left of a satin nightgown was laid out spread-eagle. Blood covered everything around the bed, and a bloody mess covered the night stand on the left. The room was otherwise undisturbed; jewelry and money lay untouched on the dresser, and the closet doors were closed.

"Her assistant found her?" Wayne asked. "What did she say?"

"Doctor Myers never missed a day," Ragland said. "So everyone at the clinic knew something was wrong."

"Then why didn't they call the police?" Wayne commented. "Hindsight?"

"Yeah," Ragland agreed. "Anyway, Ms. Brody volunteered to come by on her lunch run. She said the door wasn't quite closed so she came in. When the doctor didn't answer her calls, she headed for the bedroom, thinking maybe she was asleep, and found this."

"Ms. Brody didn't see anyone else?" Wayne asked.

"No," Ragland told him. "And the doctor's car is missing. I put out a BOLO."

"Could it be in the shop?" Sara asked. "We shouldn't assume that the killer took it."

"Good point," Nick said. "Especially if he arrived in his own car or even by taxi, and walked the last block or so."

"I'll look into that," Roth said as he left the room.

"The assistant M.E. is waiting outside to take the body when you're done." Ragland said. "He said this was done early this morning."

"No sign of forced entry anywhere?" Nick asked.

"No." Ragland shook his head. "Either he had a key or she let him in."

"So someone she knew, trusted," Wayne said.

"The assistant said that the doctor went to fund-raising functions, but really didn't have a lot of friends, including her employees," Ragland said. "It seems the doctor's not very social with anyone, especially not her ex-boyfriend; a Richard McCann. They broke up two weeks ago, according to the assistant."

"Another red herring?" Nick asked Sara.

"Could be," Sara told him. "I don't think the killer would be that obvious."

"Unless he's taunting us," Wayne said.

"We shall see," Nick said as he gave the room another once-over. "Like Sara, I think that this might be his 'unfinished business' or at least part of it."

"What is this 'unfinished business' stuff that you're talking about?" Ragland asked.

"The killer left us a note," Wayne told him. "Saying he had unfinished business that he had to take care of before he left."

"We need to have a briefing if we're going to be working a task force together," Ragland said.

"We weren't told about any task force," Nick said.

"David says that the Logan police commissioner has been talking to our section chief," Wayne said, "about that very thing. It seems the detectives' requested to start one."

"Not me," Ragland said, holding his hands up defensively.

"I'd willingly let the Kester County sheriff take the case off my hands if asked."

"Yarnell," Nick said.

"She really wants to be with you," Wayne said. "I wonder if she's coming back with us to Debow."

"Not in the SUV," Nick said.

"And she's sure not staying at my apartment," Sara said. "Which means the hotel with you, Agent Wayne."

"You might as well call me Elliot," Wayne said.

"Elliot," Sara nodded to him.

"Yarnell could cause a problem with her narrow-mindedness," Wayne said.

"I know," Nick frowned.

"If she goes, the Commissioner will probably send me as well," Ragland said. "He won't want an 'incident'."

"So why would he send her in the first place?" asked Wayne.

"Her father is his best friend." Ragland shrugged.

"She complains to daddy and daddy talks to him," Wayne said. "That about it?"

"Yeah," Ragland paused as his partner slipped into the room. "What'd you get, Roth?"

"I found out where she takes her car, and it's there," Roth said. "Seems it stopped working yesterday, and she dropped it off last night."

"So the killer didn't take it," Nick commented. "What about a taxi?"

"I called the main cab companies, but they reported that no one was picked up or dropped off within two blocks of here between midnight and six this morning. A taxi dropped her off at seven last night. Of course, there are a few smaller cab companies, but they don't all keep good records so..." Roth shrugged. "I'll call them, but odds are they won't know for sure if there was a pick up or not."

Ragland's phone rang and he stepped aside to answer it just as Yarnell entered the room. Yarnell moved to stand next to Nick, standing well within his personal space.

"I'm to work with you, Agent Issaro." Yarnell paused. "Can I call you Nick?"

"No." Nick said. "After we have a look at the initial report on

Kraig's apartment, we're returning to Debow."

Yarnell pursed her lips, but before she could say anything, Ragland rejoined them.

"That was the captain." Ragland said. "Yarnell and I are to return with you to Debow and brief each other. We're to work with you and liaison through our partners with our department."

"I can be ready in two hours," Yarnell said to Nick.

"You going to pick me up?" Ragland asked her almost innocently.

"What?" Yarnell said startled.

"Well, it's either your car or mine," Ragland said.

"I thought we'd ride with the agents," Yarnell said, looking at Nick.

"No," Nick told her.

"Why don't you and Ragland go pack," Wayne said. "And we'll see you in the sheriff's office later."

"That's a good idea," Ragland said. "I think we should take your department car to Debow, Yarnell. Agreed?"

"I suppose so," Yarnell said as she allowed Ragland to lead her out of the room.

"Good luck," Roth said before he followed the other detectives out.

"She's going to be disappointed later when she realizes that you ain't going to be at the hotel where she'd have access to you after hours," Sara said. "You should take her up on her offer and get a free meal."

"Her blood's probably bitter," Nick said.

"He doesn't like people who abuse their power," Wayne said.

Sara felt that there was more to it, but let it slide. "So, we going to swing by Kraig's apartment and get the report from the CSU people?"

"Yes," Nick said. "I don't think there will be any sign of forced entry present either, though."

The three of them left the bedroom, and Nick headed them towards the man standing in the living room with a clipboard. Nick waited until the man looked up before he spoke.

"You the Assistant M.E.?"

"Yes," the man said. "Are you done? Detective Roth said he thought you were."

"We're done," Nick said. "I wanted to ask you if you noticed anything unusual on the body."

"Not on the body, but the womb was slashed unusually." The man paused. "I called the Doc, and he said the others were not slashed this way."

"What was different about this one?" asked Wayne.

"These slashes form a five pointed star," The assistant M.E. said. "The others were slashed multiple times but no pattern."

"Alright," Nick said. "Anything else?"

"Just that she was alive when she was cut open. Can I take the body now?"

"Yes. Thank you," Nick said.

With a nod, the assistant M.E. left them, heading out the apartment door.

"Well, seems the killer knows we're on his trail," Wayne said.

"He must have drugged her," Nick said. "I didn't see any signs of ligature on her neck."

"And neither the assistant M.E nor the detectives mentioned it," added Wayne. "Nor did they say anything about blunt force trauma. The slashes though. Does the star signify something, Sara?"

"The true five elements."

"Five? I thought there was only four," Wayne said.

"There is a fifth--Aether or spirit that is formed when the others are all present. The killer has knowledge he shouldn't have."

"Let's get the initial report for Kraig's apartment and head back to the sheriff's office," Nick said. "I want to look over those medical reports and confirm Sara's theory about the abortions."

"It would give us part of the why," agreed Wayne as they headed toward the door. "And David may have some info for us by the time we get back to Debow."

The assistant M.E. passed them at the door with a stretcher. Nick put his hand on Sara's back and escorted her out of the building with Wayne following behind them. When they got to the SUV, they separated and slid into the vehicle.

"Have David do a check on Ragland," Nick said as he started the vehicle.

"Already on it," Wayne said, tapping his phone. "I'll also tell the sheriff to get two rooms for our liaisons."

"Good idea," Nick replied as he pulled into the street. "Away from you perhaps?"

"I wish," Wayne snorted. "I'll talk to the boss later tonight to see if we can get them returned to Logan."

"The killer's got ties to Logan; either he lives there or has social ties there," Nick said. "Them coming to Debow is purely for Yarnell's personal reasons."

"She definitely wants to get into your pants," Sara said. "I don't think the case is even on her radar."

"Well, it better be," Nick said. "I won't hesitate to file a complaint if she steps out of line or is too unprofessional."

"With her father friends with the police commissioner that might not go very far," Sara said.

"He won't sweep a federal complaint under the rug," Nick said.

"He might try," Sara told him. "Since he's already swept two complaints under the rug, he might not want a new investigation started."

"That's when you drag in the threat of the press," Wayne said.

"We'll see what happens." Nick pulled in behind a CSU van and parked. "Hopefully, Yarnell will be professional."

"Like she's been?" Wayne snorted before opening the back door of the SUV. "Did you want me to get the report or did you want to look at the apartment?"

"Get the report," Nick said. "You can read it on the way back."

"Right," Wayne said as he got out of the SUV. "Be right back."

"You still think there won't be anything probative here?" Sara said as Wayne disappeared on the other side of the van.

"No." Nick shook his head. "The killer's been very meticulous. Like you, I think Wells was his mistake, but the rest...no."

"The way to catch him is going to be through the link to Wells," Sara agreed. "The church and the charity functions."

"There was the scent at the church," Nick said. "Though it won't stand in court, I know that odor was at the crime scene."

"Exactly," Sara nodded. "Either one of those three men is the killer or the killer was there recently."

"I can't bring any of them in just on an odor." Nick shook his head. "Not enough probable cause."

"What about the charity connection?"

"That gives us enough to officially look into the whereabouts of the people on the lists and perhaps Father Martin, but not the other priests."

"I noticed you said officially," Sara smiled.

Nick returned her smile.

"The head tech didn't make an official initial report yet," Wayne said, sliding into the back seat. "But she did send me a text with her notes, and gave me a brief verbal report."

"Good," Nick said, starting the vehicle. "Give it to me even briefer."

"Alright," Wayne paused as Nick pulled into the street. "It's like she left voluntarily. No forced entry. Nothing out of place. Neither her purse nor phone anywhere in the apartment."

"Can we go through a drive-thru before heading back?" Sara asked in the sudden silence after Wayne's words. "It will be mid-afternoon when we get back, and we'll be stuck reading files for a while."

"I saw a burger place on the way in," Nick said. "That okay with you two?"

"Sure," Wayne said. "As long as you're buying."

"I agree with that," said Sara with a laugh.

"You both know I get reimbursed by the Agency, right?" Nick commented.

"Of course," Sara laughed. "But it's fun to make you pay up front."

"Ain't that the truth," Wayne laughed. "Especially food you don't like."

Nick pulled into the drive-thru, and let them order, paying at the window. He handed them their food, then pulled out into traffic heading for Debow.

CHAPTER NINE

"Two hours and thirty minutes," Wayne said. "You're slipping."

"Shut it," Nick told him as he pulled into a parking spot in front of the sheriff's office. "I was thinking."

"Whatever," Wayne said back.

"I was thinking," Nick said, "That if the killer murdered an abortion doctor here, what about at the two other locations?"

"Mmm." Wayne pulled out his phone and tapped on it for a bit. "I'll have David check and see if any doctors went missing in the surrounding cities of the dump sites."

"A few of them might have induced a miscarriage," Sara said. "Both abortion and induced miscarriage would qualify as 'denying their gift' if the 'gift' is creating life."

"David's having one of his minions look," Wayne said, still looking at his phone. "Oh, and Vernon is on one of Heasley's volunteer lists. The list is eight years old. That church hasn't updated its volunteer files since then."

"Is it the same church Wells worked at?" Nick asked.

"No," Wayne told him.

"Are you all coming in," came the sheriff's voice as he leaned in at the driver's side window. "You've been sitting out here for a spell."

"Is there a fresh pot of coffee inside?" Wayne asked.

"Becky made some about an hour ago," the sheriff said before stepping away from the vehicle. "Those medical records are here."

"Excellent," Nick said as the three of them got out of the SUV.

"I also got those rooms for our 'guests'," the sheriff continued as he led the way into the office. "I left the reservation open-ended."

"I'll be sending them back as soon as I can," Nick said as they all nodded to Becky at the desk.

The four of them headed on into the conference room and moved toward the table. Wayne made a detour to the coffee pot though before joining the others at the table. Sara and Wayne sat down, but the sheriff and Nick remained standing.

"Depending on when they left, we have one to two hours before the Logan detectives get here," Nick said as he shifted through the new files on the table. "So let's get to reading."

Each grabbed a folder, and started flipping through them.

"This one had a miscarriage in her second trimester," Sara said after a few minutes. "The doctor suspected that it was induced."

"An abortion for this one," Wayne said. "And it seems she had one before."

"The doctor notes show that this one was pregnant," Nick said. "But after two months there's no mention of the pregnancy. Nothing at all."

"She probably did an abortion on the sly," Sara said as she set the one file aside. "So no one would know she was even pregnant."

"Could be," Nick agreed.

"Another abortion on this one," Wayne said as he flipped though another file. "Both were done at the same clinic."

"David might want to narrow his search for the missing doctors to that clinic," Nick said.

"The doctor of this one thinks the woman induced her miscarriage as well," the sheriff said as he closed the file he held. "Also there were two abortions noted here."

"Sheriff." Dan came in, carrying a box which he set on the table. "Jack Howard just dropped this off. He said these are records from the Inn ten years ago."

"Thanks, Dan," the sheriff said with a nod to the deputy. He took the lid off the box as the deputy left and looked at the registry books, pulling one out. "They all got dates on them."

"When was Mayer here?" Nick asked.

"May of that year," the sheriff said as he pulled each book out enough to look at the dates. "We had found records of him staying the week before in Logan, but nothing the week we caught him."

"I'd stay somewhere under a false name," Sara said. "Why lead someone directly to me?"

"Ah," the sheriff said as he pulled out a book and opened it, flipping through the pages. "Here we go...six people stayed at the Inn that week; two couples and two men."

"Well, we can eliminate the couples," Nick said.

"What were the two men's names?" asked Wayne as he pulled out his phone.

A John Graham and an Arthur Hoss," the sheriff said. "There's a notation next to Hoss' name. Plus one, it looks like it says."

"Arthur Hoss, Wells' boss?" Wayne commented. "That's interesting."

"Probably an affair," Nick said with a grunt. "He struck me as that type."

"You think he was having an affair with Wells?"

"Or one of the other women at his firm. Have David check his finances for other such expenditures." Nick waved it away dismissively. "However, this John Graham. I'm guessing he is Mayer."

"I'll have David look and see if there is a John Graham," Wayne said. "and if he ever vacationed here."

"Good," Nick said. "Does he have anymore on the lists?"

"He sent a text a few minutes ago saying he didn't find any corresponding names besides Vernon's, but he said that doesn't mean there isn't," Wayne said, tapping his phone. "People don't always use their own names, as we know."

Sara gave a snort, but Nick merely raised an eyebrow.

"He's got his minions doing checks on all the names on the volunteer lists, of course, but nothing suspicious so far," Wayne said.

"What's this list business?" the sheriff asked.

"We found a link between Vernon, Kraig, and one of the local Catholic churches." Nick said. "Vernon and his girlfriend Misty

Wells volunteered at the same church Kraig went to."

"And the other body may be Vernon's girlfriend," Sara added.

"David just sent me another text." Wayne paused. "He says we should find this interesting…Father Martin was the assistant pastor in the church that Wells worked for six years ago. He still has family there which he visits regularly."

"That is interesting," Nick said. "What about Father Clarke?"

"He was the pastor of a church in a town near the Nevada dump site fifteen years ago." Wayne said. "He's gone on a couple of sabbaticals since then, the last one two years ago. David says he can't find records for those times."

"And Arthur Hoss?" Nick asked.

"Divorced businessman," Wayne said. "David says he goes to Las Vegas every year at least twice. He can't find a Wyoming connection yet."

"There might not be one," the sheriff said. "Some things are simply random."

"The other two priests are local, and have no suspicious backgrounds that David could find." Wayne continued, "No outside of town trips except to the seminary."

"Are these men suspects?" the sheriff asked.

"Three of them are," Nick said. "I smelled a scent from the cabin in the church with the three men present, but the other odors present interfered with me pinpointing it."

"When the Logan detectives get here we will give a briefing," Wayne said.

"Alright," the sheriff said as he laid the registry book on the table and moved the box aside. "The Logan police told me about the abortion doctor. You think the killer is angry that these women essentially killed their babies, and the doctor did it for a living?"

"He mentioned a mission in his letter," Nick said. "That mission has to have something to do with this."

"Sheriff," the deputy paused in the door, "the two Logan detectives are here."

"Bring them on in, Dan," the sheriff told him.

The deputy turned and gestured, allowing Ragland and Yarnell to pass him into the room. Both detectives paused just inside the door before Ragland headed for the coffee pot while Yarnell moved toward Nick.

"You made good time," Wayne commented. "I figured it'd take you time to get ready."

"Yarnell drove." Ragland grimaced. "And I always have a to-go bag ready."

Sara noticed that Nick shifted away from Yarnell when she made a move to stand in his personal space, and hid a smile at Yarnell's frown. Yarnell must be getting frustrated in her lack of progress by now.

"Let's get this briefing started," Nick said. "A couple of years ago, a body was found by some hikers in Wyoming, and more remains were discovered thereafter. Mummified remains were discovered last year in the Nevada desert with the same M.O. We put out a notification to contact us if anymore were found that had the same mode of killing; strangulation combined with mutilation of the female genitalia. The sheriff contacted us a few days ago as you know."

"These bodies were fresher and gave us additional information about the killings," Wayne continued when Nick paused. "We now suspect the reason the killer chose them was that he thought each of the women either had abortions or induced miscarriages."

"As you know, the one body was identified as Kraig, and we suspect the other body to be Vernon's girlfriend, Misty Wells," Nick said. "Vernon's tongue being cut out leads us to believe that he lied to the killer, maybe about his girlfriend. Both Vernon and his girlfriend volunteered at the Catholic church that Kraig belonged to. It would be a good way to meet the victims; through the church's volunteer and charity network. A network run by a Father Martin and overseen by a Father Clarke."

"When we went to see the two Fathers to talk to them, there was a third man present, a Mr. Arthur Hoss, who is Ms.Wells' boss," Wayne added. "All three went to the top of our suspect list…"

"Two priests," Yarnell laughed. "You've got to be kidding."

"We are not," Nick said, his voice devoid of amusement.

Ragland's phone rang, breaking the tension, and he stepped away to answer.

"Our tech is running a check on the three men," Wayne said after a few more minutes of silence. "We have found ties to Nevada and Wyoming, but nothing overly suspicious yet."

"That was Roth," Ragland said as he rejoined them. "They found Kraig's car at a mall not long after we left. CSU looked it over but didn't find any signs of struggle, her purse, nor her cell phone."

"Did they find any indications of how long it's been there?" asked Nick.

"It could only be a day or two since a BOLO was put out when she went missing," Ragland said. "But Roth said he'd fax us the report when CSU completed it."

"Alright," Nick said.

"So the killer is murdering women he thinks have gotten rid of their babies," Ragland said. "You think he killed Myers because she does abortions?"

"That's the theory," Nick told him.

"He thinks he's on a mission," Wayne said.

"Then he may go after the other doctors," Yarnell said with a frown.

"As Sara had mentioned to you," Nick said.

"Why is the local charlatan here?" Yarnell asked

"Yarnell," Ragland warned in a hard voice.

"Sara is a verified consultant," the sheriff said. "Highly valued by me."

"Doesn't mean she's not a charlatan," Yarnell said.

Sara shook her head. She suspected Yarnell was seeing her as competition for Nick's attention, and was trying to get rid of her.

"You will be returning to Logan tomorrow," Nick said. "Ragland may stay here. I'm sure the sheriff won't mind lending a deputy and a car to escort you back."

"It will be my pleasure," the sheriff told him.

"Let's be reasonable and talk about this over dinner," Yarnell said as she stepped closer to Nick. She reached out a hand to touch him, but he took a step away from her which caused her to frown. "Agent Issaro–"

"I've tried to be polite," Nick interrupted. "But you don't seem to take the hint."

"She never does," Ragland said. "Are you going to file a complaint?"

"I'm sure there's been a misunderstanding," Yarnell began.

"When the case is over, I plan to talk to the police

commissioner," Nick told Ragland, ignoring Yarnell.

"He sent me along to try to minimize any damage she did," Ragland said. "Her father works in the Mayor's office, and is the commissioner's best friend."

"Just wait 'til I speak with Father, Ragland," Yarnell told him.

"Perhaps I'll speak with the Mayor as well," Nick said. "Make sure he understands the situation."

"You'll leave after the case is over," Yarnell said.

"I won't," the sheriff told her.

Yarnell made a gesture as if dismissing his words.

"I think we should talk to Logan's internal affairs personally," Wayne said.

"I agree," Nick said. "Sheriff, why don't you have a deputy escort her to get food, then to the hotel?"

"Give me the keys first," Ragland said as he held out his hand to Yarnell.

"This is not over." Yarnell threw the keys at Ragland, and left with the sheriff.

"You know she'll be on the phone to her father within the hour," Ragland said.

"I'll talk with the police commissioner tonight when I get to the hotel," Wayne said. "I'll make it plain we're not working with her and why."

"We will still be speaking with internal affairs before we leave," Nick said.

"I'll convey that as well," Wayne told him.

"Good," Nick said with a nod. "Now back to the case."

"Dan's taking her," the sheriff said as he returned. "I told him not to let her out of his sight until she's in her room."

"We suspect the renter of the cabin, where Vernon was found, to be stalking Sara," Nick told Ragland. "He would be a good fall guy for the murders as he is the nephew of serial killer Richard Mayer. Mayer was captured here ten years ago and recently died in prison. We think the nephew Robert Kirkland has been stalking Sara since his uncle's death, but to what purpose we are not sure."

"So you think he blames her for his uncle's incarceration and later death?" Ragland asked.

"Probably." Wayne replied. "The timing's right."

"Mayer blamed me and thought I was a witch," Sara said. "He

probably passed that belief to his nephew."

"'Thou shalt not suffer a witch to live'" Wayne said.

"Exactly," Sara nodded.

"I finally got the report this morning from the tech about your car, Sara," the sheriff said. "He said he had to run a few tests before he could make the report."

"So it wasn't just a bomb," Nick said.

"No." The sheriff shook his head. "The tech said the bomb was designed to disable the car, not blow it up. He thinks that whomever put it on her car just wanted to cause her to drive off the road so she would be prime for a kidnapping."

"Probably wanted to torture me before killing me," Sara said.

"Or he wanted to take you to the site of his uncle's killings to do the deed," Nick said.

"Bomb?" interrupted Ragland.

"A bomb was found on Sara's car the day she helped us at the dump site," the sheriff said. "We suspect Kirkland of that."

"There were no fingerprints?" asked Wayne.

"No." The sheriff shook his head. "It was clean. The tech thinks the builder and whoever installed it wore latex."

"Too bad," Wayne said. "We'd be able to say for sure if Kirkland did it with prints."

"I'm sure he planted the bomb," Sara said. "The person who messed with my car was the same person who was at the dump site. With the Sinq messing up my reading at the cabin and the barn, I can't tell for sure those instances were Kirkland, but who else can it be?"

"True enough," Nick said.

"Sinq?" asked Ragland. "I'm not familiar with that term."

"Unless you're knowledgeable about the paranormal, you wouldn't have heard it much," Sara said. "It's what psychics call a null or blank. Someone who cannot be read, mentally or emotionally, who doesn't give off psychic energy. They absorb energy, but don't give it off."

"So the killer is a Sinq?" Ragland asked.

"Yes," Sara nodded. "The void echo he radiates interferes with my readings."

"A couple of my colleagues told me about you," Ragland said. "They said you're the real thing."

"I'm not a psychic, but what I do is real," Sara told him.

I'll just go with psychic," Ragland said.

"David just texted me," Wayne said as he looked at his phone. "He says he ran a statewide search in Wyoming and Nevada for doctors that were either missing or murdered. There were quite a few so he narrowed it down even further, and found twelve that would fit the criteria he used."

"Twelve?" asked Ragland. "How far back did he go?"

"Fifteen years," Wayne replied. "Two of the twelve are from a city near the Wyoming dump site and one a hundred miles from the Nevada location."

"All women's clinics?" asked Nick.

"That was one of the criteria." Wayne said. "Hospitals and clinics that specialized in women's problems. He says that he'll send us a report tomorrow."

"Good." Nick paused. "Do you have anything to add to this briefing, Detective Ragland?"

"Doctor Myer's ex-boyfriend is out of town and has been for the last week," Ragland said. "Roth is running checks on the more vocal of the anti-abortion activists, even though you don't think they have anything to do with this. He told me he'd have something for me by tomorrow morning."

"Since we have to wait, why don't we all head out and get some sleep," Nick said. "And start fresh tomorrow."

"Sounds good to me," Wayne said. "I still have to talk to the police commissioner before I can rest though."

"Don't forget to come by with a fresh change in the morning," Nick said.

"I get no sympathy," Wayne said.

"Wait 'til you get back to the hotel," Sara said. "and Yarnell finds out Nick's not going to be there."

"I don't know which is going to be worse," Wayne said. "Her or the talk."

"Her." Nick moves and holds out his hand to Sara. When she took it, he pulled her to her feet, and directed her toward the door. "Make sure Ragland gets some food before you take him to the hotel."

"Right." Wayne sighed. "Goodnight."

"I'll see you tomorrow, Agent Issaro, Sara," the sheriff called after them as Nick escorted Sara out of the room.

Sara and Nick continued on through the lobby and out the front door. At the SUV, they separated and got into the vehicle. They remained silent as Nick started the vehicle and pulled out into the street.

"Did you want anything from the café?" Nick asked as he headed towards her apartment.

"I'm not really hungry, and I've got ice cream at home," Sara told him.

"Okay," Nick said. "So you've never worked with Ragland and his partner?"

"No." Sara shook her head. "I've worked with two of his younger colleagues, and a few missing person detectives as well as a task force a couple of years ago. My gift's not as useful in the city as it is for the sheriff."

"You have other contributions," Nick said. "Besides your gift."

"It's nice of you to say so," Sara said.

"I mean it," Nick told her. "Which is one of the reasons I want to offer you a full-time consultant job myself."

"What?" Sara stared at him in shock. She hadn't expected that when he told her to hold off on giving the sheriff her answer. She had figured he wanted her to sign up with the FBI part-time, working for the sheriff in between.

"Just think about it," Nick said as he pulled into the parking lot of her apartment building. "You don't have to give me an answer until this case is over."

"Okay," Sara said before they both slid out of the SUV. "I don't know what to say anyway."

Nick stopped on the sidewalk and motioned for her to move behind him.

Before Nick could do anything else, a man straightened from behind a nearby car with a gun in his hand. The man pointed the weapon at Nick and pulled the trigger twice, causing Nick to fall to the ground.

"Nick!"

CHAPTER TEN

"Stay where you are," the man said as Sara moved to kneel beside Nick. When she straightened, he stepped onto the sidewalk. "Now I can kill you without interruption."

"I gather you're Kirkland," Sara said.

"And you're the witch who bespelled my uncle," Kirkland said.

"He was a serial killer long before he met me."

"Whatever. I had planned for you to join the bodies in the field, but bullets will do the job just as well."

"Your uncle killed me, but I didn't stay dead," Sara heard herself say over a pounding heart, anticipation and fear causing it to race. "What makes you think shooting me will work?"

"A bullet through the brain will kill anything." Kirkland raised his pistol.

In almost a single motion, Nick rolled and fired his own weapon. Sara watched the shock and disbelief flow across Kirkland's face before it went slack.

As Kirkland fell to the sidewalk, Nick sat up and took the hand Sara extended. He carefully stood, then moved to kneel by Kirkland.

"Is he dead?" Sara asked as relief flooded her. She had thought Nick was unconscious and seriously wounded. Silver bullets were just as deadly to vampires as regular bullets were for normal humans.

"Not yet." Nick sat on the sidewalk next to Kirkland and pulled out his phone. "Elliot, Kirkland showed up at Sara's. We need an ambulance and the sheriff. I need a change of clothes as well."

Sara watched as he slipped his phone back on his belt, then ran a hand over his bloody shirt. Relief was making her light-headed. "I was afraid he might have silver bullets, and you'd go into anaphylactic shock."

"The bullets fragmented and body trauma caused my reaction," Nick said. "Otherwise I would have stayed upright."

"You think the killer had anything to do with this?" Sara asked.

"I smelled blood, and Kirkland's wrists are raw and bloody," Nick told her. "Also I can see blood drops leading away."

"You're going to need blood," Sara said. "I can have one of the clinic's people drop some off."

"This isn't how I was going to do this," Nick said as he moved to stand in front of Sara, his hands going to her face. "I was going to wait until the case was over."

"What are you doing?" Sara asked, trying to step back, but Nick held her still.

"This," he murmured before touching his lips to hers. Nick held her still until she relaxed into the kiss, and deepened it when she opened her mouth. He slipped his tongue over hers, and they tangled. Once he explored her mouth and she was breathless, he pulled back and ran his thumbs over her cheekbones.

"You want me as a companion?" Sara asked, breathless.

"No." Nick shook his head. "I want to share blood."

"What?" Sara's eyes flew to his, feeling that familiar jolt as she did so.

"You are my mate," Nick said. He released her face and stepped back as vehicles entered the parking lot. "We will discuss this after the others have left."

"Are you going to be okay until then?" asked Sara.

"If you would allow me," he said, taking her wrist in his hand. At her nod, he bit into her wrist and Sara felt him drink.

It was chaos around them for a few seconds before everyone

sorted themselves out.

"Sara?" Wayne asked as he broke off from the paramedics who were working on Kirkland and moved to her side.

"I'm fine," Sara said as she felt Nick lick her wrist. "Nick was shot."

"I gathered that," Wayne said, taking in the bloody shirt. "We had just gotten to the hotel when you called."

"I think the killer left Kirkland here to kill Sara," Nick said as he stepped away from Sara. "I thought I saw a blood trail."

"There is," Ragland said as he joined them. "I noticed it and have a deputy following it now."

"Good." Nick paused as the sheriff joined them. "Well?"

"They're taking him to our medical center, but they haven't been able to stabilize him," the sheriff said. "He'll be airlifted to Logan, but I don't hold much hope. You got him in a lung and he's not stopped bleeding."

"What exactly happened?" Wayne asked.

"I smelled blood so we stopped, and he came from around a car with his gun out," Nick said. "He fired two shots, thinking he was taking me out, then moved closer. I rolled and fired, then called you."

"I'll have to take your shirt and your pistol," the sheriff said. "You do have a back-up, right?"

"Of course," Nick said as he slipped off his shirt, revealing a smooth, nearly hairless chest. He unclipped his pistol and handed both shirt and gun to the sheriff. "When your people are done, just throw the shirt away."

"Right," the sheriff motioned to the deputy photographing near by. "Ron."

The deputy came over with two evidence bags and bagged the shirt and gun. "Oh, Wes followed the trail to the bushes. There was a length of rope and a backpack, both bloody. He said it looked like maybe this guy was tied up and cut himself lose. I have Wes guarding the area until I can get there."

"Good." The sheriff paused as the deputy moved away. "So the killer left him here to work his way free and wait for you."

"Seems like," agreed Nick.

"Now all we have to figure out is if he knew you were a vampire and would kill Kirkland," Wayne said. "Or if he meant for both of you to die."

"Either way he figured we'd get Kirkland for all the murders," the sheriff said.

"Without me to disagree he would be the logical candidate," Sara said. "And everyone but the sheriff and Elliot would think the case closed."

"And they'd put down our disagreement to trauma, no doubt," Wayne said.

"Exactly," the sheriff said. "But if he knew Agent Issaro was a vampire, then this was the perfect way to get rid of a liability and muddy the trail."

"We'll have to ask him when we catch him," Wayne said before looking at Nick. "I grabbed your to-go bag. Didn't think you'd mind casual this time."

"It will be fine," Nick told him before Wayne left the group. "I think a deputy should be stationed outside for the night."

"I agree," the sheriff said. "We don't know what the killer's game plan is. This could be to lull us."

"This I believe was to muddy the trail at the very least," Nick said. "And the start of something else at the worst."

"More murders?" Ragland asked.

"Or he may move on to someplace else," Nick replied. "There's at least two other places he's killed, one not long ago, so he's not tied down by conventional means."

Wayne rejoined them with a large bag which he handed to Nick. "Your back-up's in the bag. I texted David."

"He have anything more on those concerned?" Nick asked.

"Not at this moment," Wayne said. "He did want to know if you wanted any help from the local field office, though. I told him not at this time."

"Good," Nick said before looking at the sheriff. "Did you need a statement from Sara tonight, sheriff?"

"Tomorrow will be fine, Agent Issaro," the sheriff said.

"Then I think I'll escort Sara inside," said Nick as he laid his hand on her back. "I think we've all had enough for tonight. Don't forget the deputy."

"We'll see you in the morning," the sheriff called out to them as Nick guided Sara toward her building. Sara could still hear the other men talking amongst themselves as she and Nick entered the building, even though she couldn't make out the words.

"You really think he'll try something again tonight?" Sara asked.

"He could," Nick said as he allowed her to go up the stairs ahead of him. "Better safe than sorry, isn't that the saying?"

"Yes." She paused. "Were you telling the truth?"

Nick stopped her on the landing and turned her until she was looking at him. He cupped her face in both his hands as he met her eyes. "You're my mate."

The electrical jolt ran through her body and a shiver shook her. Easy enough to believe him when he was touching her, but her insecurities would return the moment he wasn't.

"This is true." His lips touched hers briefly before he grabbed her hand and led her to her door. He allowed her to open the door, then once they were both inside he closed and locked it. "I would share blood with you."

There was a formalness to the words, and Sara searched his face. It was softened somehow, and his eyes almost glowed. The feelings he invoked in her she had never felt before, not even for her fiance. She touched his cheek and nodded. "Yes."

He leaned down and kissed her, deepening the kiss as she opened her mouth to him. Pulling back, he swung her into his arms and carried her into the bedroom where he sat her on the bed.

"Wait, wait," she told him, breathless, as he moved to join her. "I have something I need to say."

"Alright," Nick said, sitting on the edge of the bed.

"I can't have children," Sara told him bluntly. It had been one of the reasons her fiancé had left her after all, and she didn't want there to be any misunderstandings.

"I don't want any," Nick said, brushing his fingers across her cheek. "I just want you."

Sara swallowed hard as she heard the sincerity in his voice. Her inability to have children had been such a bone of contention that to find it didn't matter to this male was almost overwhelming.

Nick leaned down and kissed her again, his lips and tongue moving across her jaw and down her neck. He moved until he was lying beside her, and continued to kiss and lick her neck, causing her to shiver with sensation. His one hand began to stroke her side and stomach as he raised his head to speak. "What do you want,

Areessa?"

Her hand cupped his cheek and her eyes roamed his face. "You want me any way you can have me."

"Can't say I wouldn't love to make love to you," Nick told her. "But it is your call."

Sliding her hand to the back of his neck, she tugged his head down until their lips almost touched. "Yes," she breathed against his lips before deepening the contact.

Dragging his mouth from her lips, Nick didn't let it leave her skin as it moved over her cheek to the pulse beating wildly in her throat. His lips parted, letting her feel his teeth and tongue against her skin. He nipped her but did not break the skin right then, and licked her pulse point to soothe the sting.

"Nick…" she moaned.

"Shh, I've waited a long time for this," he whispered against her skin. His fingers unbuttoned her top, caressing the skin that was revealed as he went. He parted the metal snap of her jeans, then slowly drew the zipper down.

Nick's eyes glittered behind the half-lowered lids, and Sara swallowed again at the desire reflected there. Nick folded back the flaps of her jeans and eased them over her hips, lifting her a little to do so, and revealing the black bikini briefs she wore beneath. His mouth continued to work her pulse point, and sent shivers down her spine every time he nipped.

She sucked in a breath as he unhooked her front bra clasp, and cupped one of her breasts. His other hand slid down and eased her briefs down, causing her to tremble

"It's alright," he murmured. "You're beautiful."

Her hands went to his hips, and tugged, but Nick didn't move closer. Instead, he moved back and swiftly pulled off his own pants, causing Sara to tug at him again. This time he moved, sinking fully and deeply into her, and she cried out.

"Saffeer Areessa," Nick murmured against the pulse point on her throat. He braced himself with his forearms beside her head and moved in a series of sharp, deep thrusts as he nipped and licked her neck.

Sara lifted her legs so she was gripping him by the hips, and gave as good as she got, fierce passionate movements to meet his thrusts. She felt her orgasm build, then sweep over her, just as

Nick sank his teeth firmly into her neck. The pleasure shot through her and everything around her simply exploded. "Nick!"

"Areessa," Nick said as they both came back to themselves.

"What does that mean?" she asked, her voice husky, when he moved off of her.

"Beloved." A bare leg was hooked over hers, as if he needed to pin her down. His mouth opened on her lips in a hungry kiss, giving her a taste of her own blood. He leaned back and bit his own wrist, putting it against her mouth. "Drink."

Sara darted out her tongue to taste, and at that touch, Nick moaned. Opening her mouth more, she sucked on his wrist, and felt pleasure sweep through her again. She tried to follow when Nick withdrew his wrist a few minutes later, and reached out, but Nick caught her hand.

"That's enough for now," Nick told her, giving her another hungry kiss. "You need to rest now."

"Perhaps," Sara said after a moment of silence. "You can explain more about this soul mate bit."

"What do you want to know?" Nick asked as he nuzzled her neck.

"The whole deal," she told him. "You really didn't explain much."

"It is my responsibility to see to all your needs," Nick said as he continued to nuzzle her neck. "Physical and emotional."

"What about me?" she asked, her hand brushing through his hair.

"The bond between us will grow and we will know each other's needs." Nick said, laying his head on her shoulder. "You will live as long as me if we continue to share blood."

"If?"

"Some mates can't handle the life so they choose not to share," Nick said. "The vampire usually doesn't live long after their mate dies, especially if the bond is strong."

"Is there a timetable with the sharing?"

"Depends on the mates, but the bond is mostly mental once the original sharing is done," Nick told her. "Your body is already changing."

"You can feel that?"

"Yes."

"Wow." Sara paused. "Is this why you offered me the consulting job?"

"Partly," Nick said. "If you had said no, I would have stayed here."

"You probably don't even need a job, do you?"

"Not really." Nick laid his hand on her stomach. "My sect of vampires have been around since before biblical times according to our lexicon."

"I had heard there were over a hundred sects of vampires, each with different lexicons."

"Just fifty," he told her. "Most are branches from the five original clans. Mine is a direct line from the Orro Clan, or so our lexicon says. We are a rich sect in more than one way."

"Then you can afford to give me a real wedding," Sara said.

"And a honeymoon anywhere you want," he agreed.

"Good," Sara smiled. "But don't expect a short engagement. We still don't know each other."

"Vampires don't do short courtships," Nick said. "Being soul mates doesn't make us instantly compatible."

"Really?" Sara smirked

"Males are notoriously horn dogs, I believe you humans say."

"You sure you don't mind that we will not have kids?" she asked, hesitantly, suddenly serious.

"We vampires do not have the same biological need to reproduce as humans," Nick said, lifting his head up to meet her eyes. "Besides we can always adopt if you want a child. I want and need only you."

Sara cupped his cheek and studied the sincerity in his eyes. He had let down his guard and was letting her see everything. Having her was truly all he cared about.

Nick turned his head and kissed her palm before laying his head back down on her shoulder. "You need to rest. Your body's going through a lot of changes."

"I'll still be able to eat human food, right?" she asked suddenly.

"Of course." Nick laughed. "You're still mostly human."

"It's the mostly that I'm worried about."

"You'll heal faster, and your reflexes will be improved as will your senses," Nick said. "But you're still human otherwise."

"So a bullet can still kill me," Sara said. "Or a knife."

"Less likely since your body will aggressively act against you bleeding to death," Nick said. "And once the object is removed it will heal three times as fast as normal."

"So are there any changes in the vampire?" she asked, curious. He didn't answer, but she felt warmth on her shoulder where his cheek rested as if he was blushing. "What?"

"The vampire can only be sexual with their mate," Nick said, reluctantly. "I can still flirt, but not anything else."

"Is that why you didn't take Yarnell up on her offers?" Sara asked, her hand stroking his hair.

"The second I touched you, I knew you were my mate," Nick said. "No one interested me after that."

"Mmm," Sara said. "Anything else?"

"I can still consume blood from others but it won't satisfy my thirst completely anymore," Nick said. "You know blood is only part of the thirst."

"Yes, vampires are empaths of a sort," Sara replied. "You feel the emotions of the donor while you drink."

"And some of us are total empaths," Nick said. "But when we bond, the empathy goes almost to the point of telepathy. Once that happens, regular donors just are not anything but bland. Strong emotions will give us a taste, but it fades fast."

"So you're still on a high?" she said with a smile.

"Yes." He sighed. "And the bond is forming so I can still feel you."

"I don't feel anything different," Sara said.

"You will," Nick said, turning his head slightly to kiss her shoulder. "By morning the physical bond should be complete. The mental bond may take longer."

"I'll feel your emotions?"

"Each bond is different," Nick said, his head settling back on her shoulder. "You may just feel a presence or you may know my emotions. We'll find out in the morning. Now you need to sleep."

"You keep saying that," she told him.

"Because it's true. Now close your eyes and go to sleep."

Sara obediently closed her eyes, and before she could think about anything, she drifted away.

TINA RIFFEY

Sara took the suit from Wayne as she let him into her apartment. Nick had decided to go casual today and wear what had been in the bag from last night so she laid the suit over the back of one of the living room chairs. "Did you eat breakfast, Elliot?"

"Ragland and I both did," Wayne said. "I told Ragland to go on to the sheriff's office, and I'd come in with you guys."

"Good," Nick said as he came in from the bathroom wearing a button-down and jeans. Designer jeans, Sara noticed. "Did David send you anything on Ragland?"

"Yes." Wayne nodded. "He and Roth have got a 75% close rate, one of the highest in the homicide division, for the ten years they've worked together. Ragland's been in homicide for twenty-five years, and only got one write-up on file. Unnecessary force. That was ten years ago."

"Nothing else?" asked Nick.

"David said he can't find any dirt on him." Wayne shrugged.

"Good, cause I like him," Sara said. "I finished my breakfast so I'm ready whenever you two are."

"Before we go, I should tell you something, Elliot," Nick said. Sara could feel that he was a bit nervous.

"Okay." Wayne looked at Nick.

"Sara is my mate," Nick told him.

"That explains some things," Wayne said after a moment of silence. "I know the basics and the little the Bureau teaches, but what's the practical side of it?"

"I'll treat her just like a partner unless she's in danger," Nick said. "Probably a little more touchy, though."

"This why the section chief called me to ask my opinion of her?"

"I wanted her as a consultant if nothing else," Nick said. "A bit masochistic of me."

"I noticed that about you," Wayne said, flashing a smile. "I told him I liked her."

"I suppose you had David run a check on me," Sara said.

Wayne managed to look a little sheepish, but Nick just shrugged.

"What did he say?" she asked.

"Only that you left a lucrative art gallery job to come here after your fiancé broke off your engagement.," Wayne said. "David couldn't find any dirt on you either."

"And if he had found anything?" she asked both of them.

"Depends on what it was," Wayne said. "Most people should be given the benefit of the doubt."

"It wouldn't have changed my feelings," Nick said, and Sara felt the truth in his words. "You're my mate and I liked you from the first."

"Good," Sara said. "Now, are we going or what?"

"I'm waiting on you two," Wayne said as he headed back towards the door.

Sara followed the other two out of her apartment, and locked it behind her. Nick motioned for her to go before him on the stairs, and tagged along behind her. The three of them exited the building and got into the SUV.

"The deputy left at dawn this morning," Wayne said when he noticed Nick looking around the parking lot. "He called me before he left saying he did a patrol and didn't see anything all night."

"Okay," Nick said as he started the vehicle. "When did you leave last night?"

"Soon after you." Wayne paused as Nick pulled out into the street. "Ragland got a voice mail from his captain last night."

"Yarnell making trouble?" asked Nick.

"Yeah." Wayne nodded. "Ragland's to make a report about the 'incident' as well as us. Her father's making a fuss with both the mayor and the commissioner."

"You did talk to the commissioner, didn't you?" Nick asked.

"Oh, yeah." Wayne smirked. "Laid it out for him. Though the mate thing may drive it home even more, especially with the mayor."

"I'll make it plain to the mayor," Nick said.

"Ragland told me he doesn't trust Yarnell not to interfere with the investigation somehow," Wayne said, "in response to sending her back and reporting her. He said she's done it before."

"If she does, it won't be just her job I'll be after," Nick said as he pulled up in front of the sheriff's office. "She should take her suspension and leave well enough alone."

"I have a feeling it isn't going to be that easy," Wayne said.

All three of them got out of the SUV, and headed inside the sheriff's office. Once inside they stopped at the front desk where Becky and the sheriff stood.

"Morning," the sheriff said. "Ragland is in the conference room catching up on the case files."

"This came through this morning." Becky laid a file on the desk. "It's summaries of the interviews with the priests in Nevada and Wyoming."

"I had Chris go and pick up Detective Yarnell," the sheriff said with a smile. "They can 'girl talk' on the way back to Logan."

"Excellent," Nick said as he picked up the file from the desk. "Let's join Ragland in the conference room."

Sara led the way to the conference room and moved toward the table to sit next to Ragland. He had several files spread out in front of him, having put the others in piles around the table further away. She figured he was looking at the files for the ones they had identified, and separated the others into location and type. Nick had his nose buried in the file in his hand, and Wayne was heading toward the coffee pot as was the sheriff.

"Did you find anything new, Detective?" she asked him as he set the file he held down.

"The files I've read seem to point to the same killer," Ragland said. "And he seems to have been at it for a long time."

"Fifteen, twenty years according to the Nevada remains,"

Wayne agreed. "Maybe more. Any other remains would just be bones."

"Doc Hutson left a note this morning," the sheriff said. "One of the remains was partially wrapped in a tarp. By the coloration he thinks it's older than the others."

"That's the one I told you came from the sandy soil," Sara told Nick. "But I don't think it's from the Nevada dump site."

"Neither do I," Nick said. "Did the M.E. start on the remains yet?"

"He's sending the DNA off this morning." The sheriff said. "And would start the official examinations today. He said on his initial examines while he was retrieving DNA, he noticed all had broken hyoids."

"Like Doctor Hutson told me," Wayne said. "Anything else?"

"Just that the one in the tarp's twenty or more years, while the others are about two to five," the sheriff said. "The M.E. had his assistant run those tests while he was getting the DNA."

"Maybe the one in the tarp was his first," Wayne commented.

"Maybe even his wife or girlfriend," Nick said.

"I'll have them put a rush on that sample," Wayne said as he pulled out his phone. He tapped for a minute, then paused as he read something. "David says the section chief wants us to call him later."

"You can do that tonight," Nick told him.

"David capitalized the word both," Wayne returned.

"You can use the phone here," the sheriff said as he pointed to the large phone on the conference table. "You can conference it."

"We'll see," Nick said as he closed the file in his hand. "This says pretty much what I figured it would say."

"And what would that be," Ragland asked.

"The victims were active in the charities of the church," Nick said. "They gave of their time and some money, but the victims didn't talk much about their personal lives outside of the church. Of course most of them didn't have much of a social life outside of the church, except where it helped with their jobs."

"Any mention of Fathers Martin or Clarke?" asked Wayne.

"The detectives didn't ask about them," Nick said. "Just about the victims. They did note that only one priest in Nevada had been there long enough to remember those victims."

"Perhaps we should get the detectives to return and ask him some more questions," Wayne said, tapping on his phone again. "I'll have David ask them."

Dan appeared in the doorway and the sheriff joined him. They spoke in low tones for a minute with the deputy handing the sheriff a file before the deputy left. The sheriff moved back to the table and held up the file.

"DNA results," the sheriff said. "The cigarettes at the dump site match the ones from the cabin. Also the other body is Vernon's girlfriend Wells."

"Anything else?" asked Nick.

"The blood in the trunk of Vernon's car and at the gas station," the sheriff replied. "It came back to Vernon according to Dan. The official report's not in yet from your lab."

"As we suspected," Wayne said.

"I didn't see anything about Vernon's car," Ragland said.

"Chris hasn't written an official report yet," the sheriff said. "But we found both Vernon's and Kirkland's cars. Kirkland's car was spotless, but there was blood in the trunk of Vernon's."

"So Vernon was transported to the Ryder Inn in his own car," Ragland said. "After he was killed."

"That's how we see it," Wayne agreed.

"The fingerprints on Vernon's car were Kirkland's," the sheriff continued.

"No others?" asked Nick.

"Not even Vernon's," the sheriff confirmed.

"More evidence for the frame-up," Wayne said.

"Frame-up?" asked Ragland.

"The killer wants us to believe that Kirkland killed Vernon and possibly the women," Wayne said. "We would stop looking for the real killer or at least be derailed long enough for him to run."

"This is what you were talking about last night," Ragland said.

"Yes," Nick nodded. "The killer is playing a game with us."

"Now that he's killed Dr. Myers I wonder if he's finished here," Wayne said. "If she was his 'unfinished business' he mentioned in his note."

"The sheriff told me about the note," Ragland said. "You sure it's from the killer?"

"I'm sure it's the killer's doing," Sara said.

"Someone looking for attention wouldn't have delivered it to that reporter," the sheriff said. "By the way the only fingerprints on the envelope were the reporter's."

"As I thought," Nick said. "He wouldn't be lax about that."

"Yesterday you said you have suspects," Ragland commented.

"We thought since all of them were active in their church," Wayne said, "combined with no forced entry, that they met the killer through church activity."

"When we went to the church, I smelled an odor I recognized from the cabin," Nick said. "So either the killer had just been there or he was one of the three men who were there."

"David emailed me last night with some more on them," Wayne said. "Father Marcus Clarke is sixty-two years old and been a priest for over forty years. He's been in four different parishes including the one near the Nevada dump site. David still hasn't been able to track his sabbaticals."

"So we can't rule him out," Nick said.

"You really think a sixty year old man could do this?" Ragland said.

"Insanity can give you strength," Nick said. "As can religious fever."

"Father John Martin is thirty-five and been a priest for fifteen years. This is his second parish, besides the one where Wells worked. David said that he can't find anything that leads him to Nevada."

"No vacations or sabbaticals there?" Nick asked.

"No." Wayne shook his head. "All his vacations are to Wyoming."

"So we can move him down," Nick said. "To less likely."

"Arthur Hoss is forty-eight and been the head of PR for about ten years. Aside from his yearly trips to Las Vegas, all David could find is that he had an affair with Wells as well as with the other female assistant. No link to Wyoming."

"I think we can rule him out then," Nick said. "What about the other names on the volunteer lists?"

"He's still having his minions run the checks, but nothing yet," Wayne said. "David also looked into John Graham."

"What did he find out?" asked Nick.

"There are two John Grahams listed. One is a sixty-five year old man from New York who's never been out of New York state and the other is a ten year old boy in California. He said he did find a death certificate for a Jonathan Graham who died three years ago at the age of eighty in Florida though. David has a minion looking into that."

"So it's looking likely that it was Mayer," the sheriff said. "Who stayed at the Inn ten years ago."

"Yes," Wayne said. "Kirkland was following in his uncle's footsteps."

"Kirkland was here to kill Ms. Phillips then?" asked Ragland.

"Yes," Sara said. "After all I was the witch that caused his uncle to be caught and eventually killed."

"I wonder how the killer and Kirkland first intersected," Wayne said. "Did Kirkland see the killer kill Wells or Kraig or both and visited the killer? Or did the killer see Kirkland at the dump site and looked him up?"

"We'll have to ask Kirkland if he lives ," Nick said. "Or the killer when we find him."

"We do know they met up at the gas station," Wayne said. "The killer must have had a weapon to control Kirkland. Probably the same one Kirkland used."

"The serial number was scratched off, but the Logan lab managed to reveal a partial." The sheriff paused. "They said they'd call with the results when they had some."

Ragland's phone rang, and he grabbed it off his belt to answer.

"It probably won't lead us directly to the killer," Nick said. "I'm assuming Logan is like most big cities and has a black market in guns."

"It's a small market there, but yes," the sheriff agreed.

"That was Roth," Ragland said, interrupting. "I got something to tell you that you won't like at all."

"Yarnell did something," Nick said.

"She called her partner last night, wanting the phone number of St. Michaels," Ragland said. "But that's not all. Yarnell's partner didn't think nothing of that until this morning when he learned that a Father Travis from St. Michaels called saying both Father Martin and Father Clarke were missing."

"Both?" Wayne asked.

"Neither showed for morning mass," Ragland said. "And they were not anywhere in the church. The Missing Persons department is at the church right now."

"Have David pull Yarnell's phone records as well as the hotel's. While he's at it add the church's too," Nick told Wayne. "Have him fax them. I want hard proof."

"Right," Wayne pulled out his phone and started tapping. "We going to Logan?"

"After we get the fax," Nick said. "I think the sheriff should call the police commissioner though."

"I quite agree," the sheriff said. "I think I'll do it in my office though."

"Tell him we'll be visiting with him later," Nick said as the sheriff headed for the doorway.

"I'll be sure to mention that before I'm done," the sheriff said before he left.

"What did David say?" Nick asked.

"He's working on it now," Wayne said. "Top priority."

"Excellent," Nick said.

"With this development, I'd say that at least one of them is the killer," Ragland said. "Perhaps both of them did the killings."

"No," Sara shook her head. "Only one killer, though the other may know about it. Confessional, perhaps."

"Roth said he'd talk to the detectives assigned," Ragland said. "I didn't think Yarnell would jeopardize the investigation like this."

"Goes to show you never know about people," Sara said. "I knew she was furious about both the rejection and being sidelined."

"She's a spoiled brat," Nick said. "About time she realized there are consequences."

"Her father won't be able to get her out of this," Ragland said. "The Commissioner can't ignore such a breach."

Dan appeared in the doorway with a file, and Wayne moved to join him. Wayne took the file, and the deputy spoke with him for a brief moment before leaving.

"This is the phone records," Wayne said as he rejoined the others. "Dan glanced over them while they printed and highlighted an interesting number."

Nick took the file from Wayne and flipped it open, his eyes skimming the papers. He looked up after a moment and spoke. "There's a call from the church the night Vernon was killed to what I suppose is Vernon's number."

"That's what Dan said," Wayne told him. "He also highlighted Detective Yarnell's calls last night to Logan. Becky told him that the one was indeed St. Michaels'."

"You going to drive back to Logan as well, Detective?" Nick asked Ragland. "Or did you want to stay out of the line of fire."

"Oh, no I want to see this," Ragland said as he stood and moved towards the door. "I'll leave now while you wait to speak to the sheriff."

"You can catch your partner up when you get there," Wayne said.

"Oh, I will," Ragland said before he left.

"He headed back?" the sheriff asked as he slipped into the room and moved to join them at the table.

"Yeah, he doesn't want to miss the fireworks," Wayne said.

"The Commissioner tried to down play what Yarnell did," the sheriff said. "But I explained to him that not only would I file a complaint but so would the FBI. Dan made me a copy of the phone records in case your copy is 'misplaced'."

"Our section chief has been notified," Wayne said. "I'll give him a verbal report later after we've confronted Yarnell."

"I plan to have a long talk with Logan's IA while you're heading to Logan," the sheriff said. "I left a message last night about Yarnell's unprofessionalism, but this latest bit deserves a discussion."

"I agree," Nick said as he closed the file in his hand. "We need to leave so we get there in a timely manner."

"You going to try to beat two hours and fifteen minutes?" Sara asked as she got up from the table.

"That's what that means," Wayne agreed.

Nick shot Wayne a look, then gestured for Sara to head for the door. He moved to her side and laid a hand on her back, escorting her out of the room.

CHAPTER TWELVE

Nick pulled into a visitor parking spot in front of the grey, squat Logan police station, and turned the vehicle off. He looked at the ugly three-story building for a minute before turning to Wayne. "Wasn't Ragland going to meet us?"

"Yes," Wayne said. "But we're early, you know."

"There he is," Sara said as Ragland stepped out the front door.

The three of them got out of the vehicle and joined Ragland in front of the building. Ragland held up a hand to keep them from entering.

"I need to tell you something before we enter," Ragland said. "Someone gave Yarnell a heads up, and as soon as she arrived she called for a Rep and a lawyer. She's in the Commissioner's conference room with both, and denying that she did anything wrong. According to her, you're framing her because she wouldn't sleep with you."

"That's original," Wayne said. "She expects to get away with that?"

"Well, according to her, we're all biased against her." Ragland shrugged. "Besides, her father believes her. The Commissioner is being neutral right now, but her father is calling for your badge."

"Her father is inside as well?" Wayne asked.

"Yes, he arrived ten minutes ago." Ragland paused. "The

mayor is staying out of it for now, but if Mr. Yarnell has anything to say then the mayor will be stepping in."

"Well, let's get this show on the road," Nick said. "I want to get this over with so we can concentrate on finding the priests."

"Right." Ragland held the door open and motioned them through. "Go straight up the stairs to the second floor. It's the third office on the right."

Once through the door, there was a large stairway ahead, and hallways leading off to the left and right. It looked squat and ugly outside, but the interior was very dignified and stately.

Nick led them up the stairs at a fast pace and turned right at the landing. The door of the third office read simply 'Commissioner', and Nick pushed it open to reveal a very plain office.

"Good day, sir. May I help you?" asked the woman sitting at the desk.

"I'm Agent Issaro," Nick said. "I believe the Commissioner is expecting us."

"Yes, Sir, he is," the woman replied, then gestured to one of the two doors behind her. "Go right in there."

"Thank you." Nick inclined his head to the woman before leading the other two to the door. He opened it and allowed the other two to enter before he followed them.

Inside were four people sitting around an oval table with a well dressed older man standing at the window. The man who was obviously the Commissioner sat at the head of the table while Yarnell sat to one side with a man on her right and a woman on her left. Sara figured the well dressed man was Yarnell's father so that meant the other two were the Rep and the lawyer.

"It seems I'm a jilted suitor," Nick said.

"Then you admit it," the man by the window said. "You are harassing my daughter because she won't sleep with you."

"Actually it's the other way around," Nick said. "She called our suspects to cause us problems because I rejected her."

"Do you have proof of this, Agent Issaro?" the man on Yarnell's right asked.

"Yes," Nick slipped the file from under his arm and laid it on the table, shoving it toward the man. "You are the Rep?"

"Lon Miles," the man said as he reached out and took the file.

He opened it and flipped through it. "The highlighted numbers. I suppose one of them is the church's?"

"Correct," Nick nodded. "As you can see she called it last night."

"Anyone can fake phone records," Yarnell sneered. "You couldn't handle me turning you down and concocted this. Like priests would kill anyone."

The woman on Yarnell's left laid a hand on Yarnell's arm. "That's enough."

"Yeah, she might give herself away," Wayne said.

"Detective Yarnell brings up a valid point," Rep Miles said. "These could be faked."

"She's not worth the effort," Nick said. "But I'm sure IA will do a thorough investigation."

"For your accusations?" Yarnell smirked. "As you said you're a jilted suitor."

"I said you were the jilted suitor," Nick said. "Do pay attention."

"My word against yours," Yarnell said. "I think they will believe me over a stranger's word."

"Over a mated vampire's word?" Nick asked. "I think not."

"Besides you have two sexual harassment filings in your past," Wayne added.

"Vampire!" Yarnell stared at Nick as if he were an alien, seeming to not even hear Wayne.

"Are you a racist as well as a liar, Detective?" Nick asked with a raised eyebrow.

"I protest," Yarnell's father said. "He's slandering my daughter."

"Your daughter," Wayne said. "Caused her own trouble when she called the suspects last night. Her own partner can verify that she asked for the church's number when she called him."

"I told IA they could use this conference room," the commissioner said in the sudden silence. "Julian, your daughter crossed the line. I will not step into this."

"Nor should you," Rep Miles said. "I'll stay with you if you so desire, Detective Yarnell, but I can tell you that you're in deep trouble."

"This is all your fault," Yarnell said to Sara.

"Don't blame me for your own actions," Sara told her. "You had choices, and you chose the wrong ones."

The phone in front of the commissioner buzzed and he tapped a button. "Yes?"

"Sir, IA is here," Came the voice of the woman from the desk in the outer office.

"Good, have them come in." The commissioner tapped the button again. "I think we're done here, yes?"

"Yes," Nick said. "I think the rest is for IA to do."

"I'll stay for a bit," Wayne said. "And speak to IA, then I'll come find you."

"Alright." Nick nodded and turned toward the door just as it opened to reveal two men. "Gentlemen, Agent Wayne will give you a statement. Consultant Phillips and I need to start a search for the suspects."

"We understand," one of the men said as they stepped away from the door. "Good luck."

"Thank you." Nick gave them a nod and laying his hand on Sara's back, he escorted her out of the room.

Ragland was waiting for them in the outer office.

"Did you talk to the detectives looking into the priests' disappearance?" asked Nick as he and Sara fell in step with Ragland who conducted them out of the office.

"Yes," Ragland said as he led them down the stairs toward the first floor. "They searched the church with the two other priests and found a note in one of the confessionals."

"A note or a letter?" asked Nick as he and Sara followed Ragland past the front desk into the bullpen behind the staircase.

Before Ragland could answer, a female detective came up to them. Sara noticed that she looked similar to Yarnell so this must be either her sister or cousin.

"Landers, you know the captain said for you to keep away," Ragland said.

"I wanted to see the man who would let a murderer get away because of rejection," the woman said.

"At least you believe a priest could kill," Nick said. "Yarnell called the church and warned them, not me."

"My sister wouldn't cross that line," Landers said.

"Like she wouldn't sexually harass Jackson and Miller?"

111

asked Ragland, causing Landers to stalk away. "Sorry for that, Agent Issaro."

"Not your fault," Nick said. "Does she have a brother who works here too?"

"No," Ragland said as he led them to two desks where Roth was waiting. "As to the other, see for yourself."

Roth handed Nick a small evidence bag, and Nick skimmed over the note before handing it to Sara. It had no greeting or signature and consisted of only a few sentences.

"'Looks like my time here is up,'" Sara read. "'Do thank the detective for me. If you wish to find me you will have to go back to the beginning.'"

"Beginning of what?" asked Nick. "And why would he tell us how to find him?"

"To lure me to him on his ground," Sara said. "After all he did warn me away and I didn't listen. So now he wants a confrontation on his terms."

"That's why he let Kirkland go," Nick said. "But you think this is about that too?"

"Yes," Sara nodded. "If Kirkland killed me then fine, but mainly he was to muddy the waters. As to the beginning, where he was born or raised I would think."

"Then we need to figure out which one is the killer so we can find that out," Ragland said. "The missing person detectives have spoken to the other two priests and the church secretary and haven't learned anything. They were going to try the families next."

"They called me a few minutes ago, and said that Clarke didn't have any immediate family," Roth said. "Also they couldn't get hold of Martin's parents or sister."

"Did they look at the airlines or bus stations yet?" asked Nick.

"The detectives said they sent out some Unies to check, but hadn't heard back yet," Roth said.

"Does the church have a community car or does either of the priests have one?" asked Sara.

"Father Martin has one as does the church," Ragland said. "Martin's is missing and we put a BOLO out on it, but if they left last night..."

"I know," Nick said. "Hopefully, we'll find at least one of the priests."

"So what's the word?" Wayne asked as he joined them.

"Still searching for the priests," Nick said as Sara handed Wayne the note. "But that was found in the church."

"Mmm," Wayne commented as he skimmed the note. "Do we know which one wrote it?"

"No." Ragland shook his head. "You all done with IA?"

"Yes," Wayne said as he handed Ragland the note. "They told the commissioner they'd be talking to him about those two sexual harassment suits. He didn't look happy."

"He wouldn't be," Ragland said. "This could cause him more than embarrassment."

"Good," Nick said. "Did IA say anything about talking to me?"

"No." Wayne shook his head. "They seemed to be eager to talk to Yarnell in more detail though. She was still refusing to say anything when I left."

"I hope they bring home the consequences of her actions to her," Nick said. "That didn't seem to have sunk into her when we left."

"I think it started to when IA sent her father on his way," Wayne said.

Roth's phone rang and he grabbed it off his belt. "Roth...Where?...Okay."

"I think they either found the car or one of the priests," Wayne said.

"Maybe both," Sara said as Roth scribbled something down and closed his phone.

"The Unies found the car at the Municipal Airport," Roth said. "One of the airline agents remembers seeing a priest, but not if he bought a ticket or not. I'm to meet one of the Missing person detective's at the airport to question the parking lot attendant, and see if he saw the priest arrive."

"Go ahead, Roth," Ragland said. "Just keep us informed."

"Right." Roth nodded and headed out of the bullpen.

A red-headed man came up from the side and nodded to Ragland, "Ragland."

"Lorin," Ragland returned. "Detective Lorin, this is Agents Issaro and Wayne. I'm sure you remember Consultant Phillips.

Agents, this is one of the missing persons detectives assigned to the priests' case."

"Agents," the twenty something Lorin said, then turned to Sara. "Nice to see you again, Sara. You're looking good."

"Likewise, Detective," Sara said with a smile. He had been open-minded when she worked with them two years ago, unlike his partner who had thought her a charlatan until she found the body in the back yard. Some missing person cases in city suburbs ended up that way unfortunately.

"Anything new besides the airport sighting?" asked Nick as he rested his hand against Sara's back. Sara could almost feel the jealousy. He didn't like it that the man was paying extra attention to her.

"No." Lorin shook his head. "I left messages on both Martin's parents' and sister's voice mails, but nothing yet there. I couldn't find any immediate family for Clarke. I came down here for a briefing since I was told the priests are suspects in a serial murder case."

"You know the basics I'm sure," Wayne said.

"Of course," Lorin said. "When the FBI shows up, the reason spreads."

"We narrowed down that the victims were active in their churches," Wayne said.

"I think I can guess from there," Lorin said. "The priests went to the top of the suspect list when they disappeared."

"Correct," said Wayne. He took the note in its evidence bag off the desk and handed it to Lorin. "You saw this at the church."

"This does make it likely that one of them is the killer, if not both," Lorin said as he looked at the note. "No fingerprints?"

"No," Ragland said. "The lab got nothing off of it."

"CSU's initial report says that there's no sign of struggle," Lorin said. "But some clothing is missing from both rooms."

"So both left voluntarily," Wayne said.

"So it would seem," Lorin agreed. "But neither told Father Travis or Father Christopher they were leaving."

"Did the Fathers hear them talking about any trips?" asked Wayne.

"No," Lorin paused as his phone rang. "Detective Lorin…Ah, Mrs. Harris, as I said on my voice mail, I'm looking for your brother…Oh, I see…Thank you…Goodbye."

"Father Martin's sister?" asked Wayne.

"Yes," Lorin answered. "It seems their father had a heart attack yesterday and Father Martin flew in to be with him. Mrs. Harris said Father Clarke gave Father Martin the leave. She also said she'd tell her brother about my message when she returns to the hospital."

"Good," Nick said. "This makes it more likely that Father Clarke is the one we're looking for. Elliot, have David compile, then fax, Clarke's complete file to the sheriff's office."

"Will that include his childhood?" asked Sara as Wayne pulled out his phone.

"It will have every detail from birth to present that David can find," Nick told her.

"David says that he'll have it by morning due to the difficulty of acquiring some of the records," Wayne said. "Not everything is digitized, whatever that means."

"Not on computer," Sara told him. "You should know that."

"I'm not a geek," Wayne told her.

One of the IA officers from upstairs came up to them right then. "Agents, Detectives, and Ms. Phillips."

"What can we do for you, Detective Ryan?" Wayne asked as the others gave the man a nod.

"I wanted to bring you up to date," the IA detective said. "We have suspended Detective Yarnell without pay for the duration of the investigation, and she will very likely lose her job. It is up to you if you want to pursue any federal charges, but we will pursue charges of impeding an investigation at the local level. Also we are looking into the Commissioner's dealings concerning Detective Yarnell. I believe we have addressed your concerns in this."

"Yes," Nick said. "However, I believe there may be interference from Detective Yarnell's father and the Mayor."

"That will not be tolerated," the IA detective said. "I have also agreed to keep both Agent Wayne and your section chief apprised of our actions."

"Excellent," Nick said.

"Thank you, Detective," Wayne said.

"Not a problem," the IA detective said before heading out of the bullpen.

"That's one thing taken care of," Nick said. "We need to head back to Debow, and pack. We may have to fly out tomorrow."

"You want me to follow you back to Debow?" Ragland asked.

"No." Nick shook his head. "You finish up any lose ends you find here and keep us informed, but this is on us from now on. He's done here."

"I agree," Ragland said. "Lorin, we keep each other in the loop."

"I'll call you when Father Martin gets back to me," Lorin said to Ragland before turning to the two agents. "Agents, it was nice meeting you."

"Likewise, Detective," Wayne said as Nick inclined his head.

"And it definitely was a pleasure meeting you again, Sara," Lorin said with a smile at Sara. "Do keep in touch."

"We'll see, Detective," Sara told him with a glance up at Nick who was frowning at the detective. Nick was jealous again it would seem.

The detective also looked at Nick, then with another smile, he headed out of the bullpen.

"On the way back can we get some food?" Sara asked. "We missed lunch, you know."

"Burgers again?" Nick asked.

"As long as I eat," Sara said.

"Amen," Wayne said. "I'm starving."

"Alright, alright," Nick said with a little gesture. "It was nice meeting you, Detective Ragland. Do keep Elliot in the loop."

"I will," Ragland said. "It was nice meeting you all."

"I'll call you tomorrow with an update," Wayne promised as Nick and Sara moved away from the desk. He then turned and followed them out of the bullpen.

CHAPTER THIRTEEN

Sara stretched out on one of the hotel's double beds as she watched Nick remove the two suits from the closet and put them in the suit bag on the other bed. The three of them had made the drive in two hours and twenty minutes, and had headed straight to the hotel. Wayne had texted the sheriff that they were back, and he had said he'd come over for a briefing.

"You seem pensive," Nick said as he paused in his packing. "You're coming with us, you know. Not out of my sight, remember?"

"Not to mention I'm your mate," she said with a smile. "That's not what's making me pensive. I just have a bad feeling about going after him."

"Are premonitions part of your gift?"

"Not per se," Sara told him. "Since I'm connected to the earth, I'm also linked to the Aether which is where all the elements merge."

"And where the spirits mingle," Nick said. "Shaman supposedly get knowledge from there when they go into a trance."

"When shaman 'spirit walk', they are actually going into the Aether," Sara agreed. "But no I don't have actual premonitions, just 'feelings' now and then."

"So no specifics?" asked Nick. "Just a vague 'feeling'?"

"Afraid so," Sara shrugged.

"Not very helpful," he told her.

"Nope." She moved up and settled against the headboard as Nick finished his packing. "As I've said it's not always a gift, and there are limitations."

"Have you thought about what you want to do once this case is over?" Nick asked as he sat on the edge of the bed beside her. "I can take vacation time."

"I don't really know," Sara said as she reached out to take his hand. "Tell me about Nick Issaro."

It's Niccollo. Issaro was my father's name," Nick said, squeezing her hand. "I'm three hundred and fifty-two, and a billionaire."

"So you can afford a giant ring as well as a wedding," Sara said with another smile. She had figured he was at least a millionaire since most older vampires had had time to accumulate wealth.

"Yes," Nick nodded. "I have five houses and a bunch of apartments. The FBI has been my workplace for the past twenty-three years, though I've worked with three different partners in that time. Elliot being the third."

"Elliot mentioned that the one before him retired."

"I worked with Jack for fifteen years," Nick said. "Are you worried about how you would be received?"

"A little," she admitted. "I do not want to start with resentment against me."

"I can't say there won't be any. That's human nature. I can tell you that Elliot likes you, and that's all we need to do our jobs."

"I don't want to cause you trouble."

"You won't." Nick squeezed her hand again. A knock at the door caused him to set her hand on the bed and stand up. He moved to the door and let the sheriff in the room. "Sheriff."

"Agent Issaro." The sheriff gave Nick a nod, then looked at Sara. "Evening, Sara."

"Jacob." Sara drew her knees up to her chest and wrapped her arms around them. "Anything new?"

"Not on my end," the sheriff said. "But the initial report is in on Martin's car. It was wiped clean inside. Detective Lorin said according to Father Martin, Father Clarke dropped Martin off at the airport last night after Martin got the call from his sister, and Clarke wasn't acting any different than normal. And Kirkland's still unconscious."

"Did they find out if Clarke purchased a ticket anywhere?" asked Nick.

"I gave Agent Wayne the particulars, but yes," the sheriff answered. "He bought a ticket to Arizona, using his own name."

"He might have done that to throw us off his trail," Sara said. "Why buy a ticket in your name if you're on the run?"

"My thoughts exactly," Jacob said. "Detective Lorin said he'd take care of notifying the police in Arizona."

"We'll be in, in the morning," Nick said. "By that time our tech should have Clarke's information sent to your office, and we can plan our next move."

"By mid-morning we should hear something from Arizona," Jacob said.

"You already talked with Elliot?" asked Nick.

"I gave him a full report," Jacob told him. "So he's up to date."

"Good," Nick said. "He can take care of any details."

"I got a call from Yarnell's father," Jacob said. "He wants to talk to me about the complaint."

"Did he say when?" asked Nick. "Or anything else about the complaint?"

"Just when it's convenient for me," the sheriff told him. "And nothing specific."

"He's going to try to bribe you," Nick said. "Or blackmail you with some leverage he thinks he has."

"Probably," Jacob said. "I set the time for tomorrow late afternoon. We should know our next step by noon, and I can drive to Logan after."

"Noon at the latest," Nick agreed. "Did you hear anything from Logan IA as well?"

"Just the initial report earlier," Jacob told him. "About her being suspended without pay until the investigation is finished. I'm sure they'll get to my formal statement before long."

"Which is why her father called you," Nick commented.

"I don't know whether he's blind or just doing damage control," Jacob said. "But he'll find I'm not to be manipulated."

"And Detective Ryan didn't seem like he was going to let this slide," Sara said.

"The commissioner's cover up didn't sit well with him or his partner, Agent Wayne told me," Jacob said.

"Hopefully, they will come to the right resolution and not let political pressure play a part of that decision," Nick said.

"If it does, I'll see about an appeal," the sheriff told him.

"Good," Nick said. "I'll feel comfortable about leaving this in your hands then."

"I'll keep on top of it," Jacob replied. "Don't worry."

"I hope they see sense," Nick said.

"They'd better," the sheriff agreed as he turned towards the door. "Well, I'd best be going."

"Good night, Jacob," Sara said as the sheriff paused at the door. "See you in the morning."

"Oh, by the way, Agent Wayne told me to tell you that Agent Issaro has unlimited credit," Jacob said with a glance over his shoulder. "And to remind you that the jewelry store is still open for another two hours."

"I'm sure you thanked him for his concern," Sara said with a smile.

"Of course," the sheriff said. "He also said he'd talk to Agent Issaro about proper proposal etiquette."

Nick made a face at that statement, and Sara laughed. "He's your partner."

"Just wanted to warn you," Jacob said before opening the door. "Goodnight, Agent Issaro, Sara."

The door closed behind the sheriff and Nick turned to Sara. "Do you want to buy your ring here?"

"We don't know when we'll have another time to do so," Sara said as she scooted to the edge of the bed. Wayne was definitely not being subtle.

"That's not really an answer," he told her.

"Yes." She nodded, and stood up, maintaining a calm exterior even though excitement was bubbling up underneath. This would really start the tongues awaggin'. A confirmed bachelorette getting engaged, and to an out-of-towner, too. "And lucky for you the jewelry store has a wide range of engagement rings in stock."

"Then shall we go?" Nick picked up his garment bags. "We

can stop by there before we go back to your apartment."

"An excellent idea," Sara said as they headed toward the door. "You know where it is?"

"Yes." Nick followed her out the door toward the SUV. "I looked it up last night after you were asleep."

So he had been thinking about it.

Nick put his clothes in the back and got into the driver's side as Sara slid into the passenger seat. "Is there anyone you want to contact before we leave tomorrow?"

"I shot a quick text to my aunt this morning," Sara told him as he started the vehicle. "I'll call her sometime after this case is over. My parents moved to Florida years ago and I only hear from them at Christmas. There's no one else."

"Now there is," Nick said as he pulled into the street. "You'll never be alone again."

"I have been feeling strange," Sara told him. "It's like there's warmth in my head, not like a fever, but similar."

"That's the mental bond forming and strengthening," Nick said. "It will settle down once the bond is complete."

"So you're feeling it too?"

"Yes, as well as flashes of your emotions," Nick told her.

"I've been getting flashes as well. Will that change?"

"It will be more like knowing what I'm feeling at a given time," Nick said. "Not actually feeling them once everything settles."

"So you really were jealous that Lorin was being friendly with me," Sara commented with a raised eyebrow.

"You like him."

"I consider him a friend. You have no reason to be jealous."

Nick didn't say anything as he pulled into the parking lot next to the jewelry store.

"I mean it." Sara thought it was cute that he was jealous which re-enforced the excitement she was containing. She never thought she would get this far in a relationship again. "Now let's go get me a ring."

"Alright," Nick said as they both slid out of the vehicle. He joined her in front, then laid his hand on her back to escort her to the door. Leaving his one hand on her back, he opened the door with the other and guided her inside.

"May I help you?" asked the middle-aged lady behind the long glass case.

"We'd like to look at your selection of engagement rings," Nick said.

"Do you have a price range?" the lady asked as she moved along the case to the left. "We have a wide range."

"No limit," Nick said as he and Sara moved to where the saleslady was standing.

"I'd like to look at the quarter karat rings," Sara said. She didn't want to be too flashy, but she wanted a ring different from the one she'd had before.

"Alright," the saleslady reached in the case and pulled out a tray with an assortment of rings. "These are all a quarter of a karat."

"Thank you." Sara moved closer and studied the rings for a second before taking one out. It was a plain white gold band with a multi-faceted diamond surrounded by chips of amethyst. The tag even said it was in her size, and Sara smiled as she slipped it on. This was it. "I like this one."

Nick immediately pulled out his wallet and handed his credit card to the saleslady. She put the tray back in the case and headed toward the cash register with both the card and the ring as Nick turned his attention back to Sara. "I have some amethyst pieces among my collection you might like."

"Of course you'd have a jewelry collection," Sara said. "We need to have a long discussion about things."

"We will when the case is over," Nick promised. "We'll take a few days and get to know each other better."

"I'll hold you to that," Sara told him. She imagined it would take days to know just the basics about him.

"Good," Nick said as the saleslady returned with his card and a small box. He took the card she held out and returned it to his wallet before taking the small box. "You want the full deal, Areessa?"

"Just put it on my finger," Sara said, extending her hand towards him. His intent and emotions were clear; she didn't need a show. "You can wine and dine me after the case is over if you want."

"As you wish," Nick said as he opened the box. "Will you

marry me, Miss Sara Phillips?"

"Yes," Sara said, allowing Nick to take her hand and slide the ring on her finger. "Nicely done."

Nick brought her hand to his lips and kissed her fingers.

Sara could feel a warmth in her cheeks and knew she was blushing. This was the first time a man had done that and it made her feel different. Most men usually didn't pay her that much attention, at least not sexually, unless they were desperate, drunk, or doing it on a dare. She was good 'friend' material, but not partner-wise, and she was not used to it. Even her last fiancé hadn't been this way.

"As I said, you will never be alone again," Nick said with a squeeze of her hand. "You want to head back to your apartment now or do you need to do something else before that?"

"We'll be returning after the case is over, right?" Sara asked.

"For any of your belongings you may want," he agreed as he looped his arm with hers.

"Then I can tender my resignation when we come back," Sara said.

"So the apartment, then?" he asked.

"Yes," Sara nodded, then glanced at the saleslady's name tag.. "Thank you for your help, Clara."

They turned and headed toward the door, still arm in arm. Nick opened the door with his free hand, then escorted Sara outside and into the parking lot. At the SUV, they separated, and each got in the vehicle.

"You sure you don't want to get any food?" Nick asked as he started the SUV.

"Positive," Sara said as he pulled out into the street. "What about you?"

"Oh, I'm hungry," he said with a leer. "But not for food."

Warmth flooded Sara's cheeks again, and Nick laughed, causing Sara to blush even more. "Stop that, you wicked man."

Nick laughed again and reached over to touch her cheek. "You make me feel young again, Sara."

"Is that a good thing?"

"Definitely," he said, returning his hand to the wheel. "I was growing tired, but you brought me a light in the darkness."

"Many of the older vampires seem withdrawn when they come

into the Clinic. The younger ones are all chatty and always seem to be in a hurry, but the older ones…They seem to be sunk in their thoughts."

"When you live centuries, life can become weary," Nick said. "The trick is to find something that engages your interest and keeps it."

"That why you joined the FBI?"

"I had been a cop for fifty years," Nick told her. "I was near burn-out so I took some time off, then this position opened. Before I was a cop, I was a guard…I don't really know anything else."

"You wouldn't know what to do with yourself if you weren't working either, no doubt."

"I've taken 'vacations'," Nick said. "But yes, I have to work."

Sara didn't say anything as they pulled into the parking lot of her apartment building and Nick parked the SUV. She was also a workaholic in her own way, but she knew how to play too.

"I didn't mean to upset you," Nick said, turning toward her.

"You haven't," she reassured him. "I'll just have to teach you how to play."

"I know how to play," he said, his eyes running over her. "I'll show you once we're inside."

"I told you to stop that," Sara said, blushing again.

"Why would I?" he commented. "I like the response I get."

Shaking her head, Sara got out of the vehicle and headed towards the building's front door. Before she had taken a dozen steps, Nick's hand was on her back and he was walking beside her. They swept into the lobby, and Sara stopped to check her mail.

There was only one thing inside the box and as she reached in to pull it out, Nick stopped her. "Nick?"

"I smell the odor from the church," he said as he looked in the box. "It looks like a flyer from Kester County Women's Clinic."

"The one the doctor was from."

"Yes," Nick said as he reclosed her box and handed her back her keys. "We'll let Elliot collect it in the morning. I think Clarke sent it after he killed Doctor Myers and before Yarnell called him."

"Did you see any writing on it?"

"Not on the up side." He shook his head as he guided her to the stairs. He followed her up the stairs, and went in to the apartment after her. As soon as the door was closed, he pulled her to him, and pressed his lips to hers.

His eyes were dark when he raised his head, and his hands slid under her shirt to unfasten her bra. He removed both her shirt and bra, keeping her hips against his, revealing his arousal. As his fingers brushed her skin, a tremor went through her, and her own hands went to his waist to keep her upright. He removed his own shirt, and while his clever fingers unfastened Sara's jeans, she undid his..

Their jeans were shoved down at the same time, and both stepped out of them before coming back together. Nick's fingers roamed her body at will, as his mouth covered hers, and Sara wrapped her legs around his waist. Shifting, Nick slid into her, and wrapped his fingers around her hips as he turned to push her against the door.

"Nick," she said hoarse with need as he thrust into her. Passion and desire rose in both of them, and each lost control, moving erratically until their orgasms overwhelmed them.

They surfaced still clinging to each other, and Nick carefully withdrew, allowing Sara to stand on shaky legs. He kissed her softly, then nuzzled her neck, his hands keeping her close, as his fangs sank into her neck.

Sara's fingers went through his hair, and she relaxed as he drank. She had felt his orgasm as well as her own, and was still riding the 'high'.

"Areessa," Nick breathed against her neck after licking the bite closed. He bit his own wrist and pressed the wound against her lips, moaning at the touch of her tongue as she licked the flowing blood. A minute later, he pulled his wrist away and licked the wound to ensure it closed.

"How long's your recovery time?" Sara asked, having felt a twitch when she had licked the blood.

"As fast as you want it," Nick told her.

"Good," she said, grabbing his hand and leading him toward the bedroom. "Let's re-christen the bedroom then."

CHAPTER FOURTEEN

"Good morning, Elliot," said Sara as she stepped off the stairs into the lobby of her apartment building. Wayne and Nick were standing in front of the mailboxes, looking at something.

Both Wayne and Nick turned from her mail box to look at her. Wayne held an evidence bag with the flyer inside it, and waved it toward her. "Morning, Sara…This is definitely from Doctor Myers' clinic. I'll give it to the sheriff for the lab to check out."

"We headed to the sheriff's office then?" she asked.

"Yes," Nick said. "I took your suitcase to the SUV earlier, and Elliot loaded his stuff when he got here."

"I called the Sup and told him I'd be gone for awhile," Sara said. "So I'm ready."

Nick moved to her side and pulled her close to give her a brief kiss before escorting her to the front door. He waved Wayne through first, then guided Sara out into the parking lot.

At the SUV, they separated and got into the vehicle.

"I see you got her a ring," Wayne commented as Nick started the SUV.

Nick frowned at him in the rearview mirror, even as Sara laughed and turned towards Wayne. She extended her hand over the seat and allowed Wayne a closer look at the ring.

"He tell you that he has a jewelry collection to rival royalty?"

Wayne asked as Nick pulled out into the street.

"Well, he mentioned something about having amethysts in that collection," Sara said as she turned back to the front. "But nothing about how many or how big the collection is."

"And before you say anything," Nick said, "she and I will take some time off after this case and discuss things so you can stop dropping hints."

"I don't know," Sara said. "I kind of like it."

Wayne laughed as Nick gave a grunt.

"You said you called the hospital this morning?" Nick asked, obviously changing the subject. "And the doctors told you Kirkland had improved."

"They lightened his meds and he showed signs of waking up," Wayne confirmed. "They think he'll be conscious within a day or two if his vitals continue to improve."

"You call the sheriff this morning as well?" Nick asked.

"After I talked to the hospital," Wayne said. "He said he's sending a deputy to stay with Kirkland so they can question him as soon as possible."

"Excellent," Nick said. "Anything else?"

"Besides Clarke's file, David also sent the initial reports on the doctors that went missing in Wyoming and Nevada," Wayne told him. "David said he has a minion still working on it."

Nick pulled into a parking spot in front of the sheriff's office and shut off the vehicle. "Did David say anything about those sabbaticals that Clarke took?"

"Just that he was still working on it," Wayne said.

Nick grunted, then got out of the SUV with the other two. They all headed to the door and entered the sheriff's office.

"Clara said you came by last night," Becky said by way of greeting.

"Small towns," Wayne laughed.

"We're not so small," Becky said. "But I know a lot of people."

"Head on in," Nick said. "We'll be in, in a minute."

"Alright," Wayne nodded to Becky, then left for the conference room.

Sara and Nick moved to the desk, and Sara extended her hand so Becky could get a closer look at the ring. "Maybe this will spur the sheriff."

"I doubt it," Becky said with a quirk of her mouth as she studied the ring. "He's too gun shy."

"So are you," Sara told her. She knew both had had bad relationships before.

Becky inclined her head in acknowledgement.

"We'll send you and the sheriff an invitation," Nick said. "Maybe a vacation will start a change."

"We are both workaholics," Becky said. "A few days off would be nice."

"As soon as it's set, we'll contact you," Sara said. She planned to make it as soon as possible. No second thoughts for either of them that way.

"It's a date then," Becky said as the other two moved away from the desk.

Nick and Sara headed to the conference room where Wayne and the sheriff waited by the coffee pot. Jacob held the evidence bag in his hand while Wayne was sipping some coffee.

"Didn't you have enough of that this morning?" Nick asked as he and Sara entered the room.

"Never enough." Wayne moved to the table with a cup of coffee. "The sheriff said he looked over the missing person reports."

"Before we get into that, I want to say congratulations to you both." Jacob moved to the table too. "I hope you have a long life together."

"Thank you," Nick and Sara said together, making the other two laugh.

"Anyway, all three of the doctors he sent files on worked for women's treatment centers that had reputations as abortion clinics." The sheriff paused. "Your tech included reports of skeletal remains that were found within a year after the disappearances. None of the skeletons had enough to get precise DNA samples, all inconclusive, so the doctors are still considered missing."

"Were they all women?" Sara asked.

"Two of them were," Jacob said. "One of the doctors from Wyoming was a man and they found arterial spray in his home."

"So one of the remains in Wyoming may be the female

doctor," Wayne said.

"That's a possibility," Nick agreed. "Is there anything else, Sheriff?"

"Not about the doctors," Jacob said. "But DNA results are in on the remains from the dump site. Most were inconclusive including the tarp wrapped one, but two came back to missing women from Logan. The FBI lab is going to redo the inconclusive ones with fresh samples, and the Logan police are going to send me the files on the other two sometime this morning."

"Excellent," Nick said as he moved to the table with Sara and grabbed the thick folder sitting on top of the others. "I gather this is Clarke's."

"Yes." Jacob nodded as he headed toward the door. "Your tech told me that it includes some info on his parents that you might find interesting. I'm going to give this evidence to Dan. I'll be right back."

"Well, let's divide and conquer." Nick opened the folder and divided the contents before handing each person a part as the sheriff left the room. "Remember the note he left while you read."

Sara took her part of the folder and sat down at the table. It looked like she had the information about his parents and his birth.

Clarke's father seemed to have a 'normal' background with no criminal record, but his mother had some inconsistencies. She had some minor trouble with the law and missing time in her official records. Most of her trouble with the law included stints in a psych ward. Once Clarke's parents were married, things seemed to settle down with her, but there were still some odd occurrences.

The sheriff re-entered the room minutes later while the others were still reading, and moved to the coffee pot. "Did you find anything?"

"His schooling seems to be normal," Wayne said. "But there's a two year gap between high school and seminary. David made a notation that he couldn't find anything from that time at all."

"I think his mother was a Voice." Sara looked up and glanced at the other three to gauge their reaction. She wasn't sure how her words would go over.

All of them showed surprise, but Nick was the one who asked, "Why do you think so?"

"Little things in her background." She shook her head. "It

would explain how he knew about my gift. When did he join the seminary?"

"September of 1973," Wayne said.

"His mother died June of 1973 due to cancer," Sara told him. "His paternal grandfather was a priest, and probably pointed him towards the seminary."

"And he was vulnerable," Jacob said. "To that influence."

"In more than one way," Sara said. "He was probably rejected as a Voice when his mother died because of him being a Sinq. I think he might be transferring that rejection to the women he killed."

"They're killing their babies, thus 'rejecting' a 'gift'." Nick nodded. "Could be. Anything else you got from that bunch?"

"Just that he was born in North Dakota. Some town called Purcell." She laid her part down on the table. "David included a side note that there had been some kind of Indian and settler massacre nearby in the 1800's, and it's a tourist attraction."

"Tourist attraction?" Wayne frowned.

"Yeah, because of the mystery of who did it." Sara shrugged. "All the army found was dead bodies and no sign of who killed them all. Purcell was founded ten years after the massacre."

"You think this is where he means by the beginning?" Jacob asked.

"He was born there, and his mother died there which started a new part of his life," Sara replied. "Each of those was a 'beginning'."

"The seminary was a new 'beginning' too," Wayne said.

"We'll just have to check them both out." Nick looked at the sheriff. "You were gone for a while. Something happen?"

"Logan IA wants me to come in," Jacob said. "I figure I'll give my statement, then visit Mr. Yarnell."

"He won't be happy," Nick said.

"Anything he thinks he has on me will not affect my standing as sheriff," Jacob said. "Kester County may be rural, but they're not backward."

"Politicians like him and the Mayor have more to lose in mudslinging," Wayne said. "The littlest thing can cost them their offices and positions if the press gets a hold of it."

"My position is safe," the sheriff said. "You going to fly to

North Dakota first?"

"I think that would be best," Nick agreed. "Meanwhile David can get someone to check the seminary and surrounding area for any sign of Clarke so we can hit the ground running if he's there."

"Are we taking a commercial flight," Sara asked. "Or does the FBI have its own plane like in the movies?"

"Neither," Nick told her. "We flew down here in one of my own planes."

"One of your own planes," Sara echoed. Would she ever get used to these surprises? They definitely needed to have that talk.

"He's got three," Wayne said with a smile. "Two jets and the Cub we flew down in."

"I wondered how you got here so quickly," Jacob commented. "Mr. Moran also called me this morning, just after Logan IA. He told me Agent Wayne gave him a phone interview, and he wanted to get an interview with me before he ran a story."

"I told him I couldn't give him specifics on suspects," Wayne said. "But I gave him a rundown of the case and told him we were following up on leads."

"Well, I set a time for tomorrow with him," the sheriff said. "I might give him a lead on another story about an unprofessional cop if IA doesn't get its act together."

"As long as it doesn't compromise the two cases any more than they already are," Nick told him. "I want both successfully prosecuted."

"Once both cases are completed I'll have another talk with Moran," Jacob said. "A two for one deal since he was so co-operative with us."

"That's up to you," Nick said. "You're familiar with the press here."

"Oh, Sara, your car," Jacob said. "I had it taken to my place. I'll keep an eye on it until you return."

"Did you get the ticket?" she asked him. She hoped it wasn't too much.

"I paid it," the sheriff said. "After all, it was because of your work with me that you were targeted."

"Jacob..." she began, but he cut her off with a gesture.

"You know it's true so no more discussion." Jacob paused. "Besides you should get more than that small consultant fee for what you've done for this county—and me."

"Alright." Sara put her hands up in surrender since she knew when it was a waste of time arguing with Jacob.

"Do you need anything else from me before you head out?" the sheriff asked Nick. "I plan to leave soon as well."

"Just to keep an eye on things. Elliot will keep you in the loop."

"Well, I'll wish you a good flight then." .

"I'll see you when we return, Jacob," Sara said as Nick pulled her toward the door with Wayne bringing up the rear. "We'll let you know when that will be."

Becky waved to them when they swept through the lobby.

"Is there anything else you need to do?" Nick asked Sara as they made their way to the SUV.

"No, I'm good." She got into the vehicle and waited until the other two were in the car before speaking again. "So you're a pilot as well?"

Nick started the vehicle and pulled into the street before answering. "One of my cases involved flying contraband so I decided to learn the mechanics. I found I liked it."

"So you became a pilot and bought the toys," Sara said.

"Something like that." Nick paused and glanced at Wayne in the mirror. "Elliot's a pilot too."

"Don't get me in this. I'm only a beginner. I just got my license to fly the Cub. He can fly any aircraft."

"If it's worth doing it's worth doing well," Nick said. "Besides the FBI was paying."

"You're incorrigible." She laughed.

"And I'm all yours," he told her with a side glance.

"Hey, no hanky panky," Wayne interjected. "I can handle some PDAs but no sex or sex talk."

"Jealousy doesn't become you," Nick smirked.

"As if." Wayne huffed. "I like being single just fine, thank you."

Sara watched them banter with a smile. She could tell Nick liked Wayne as if he were a younger brother. The relationship between them was more family bond than partnership. She wondered if that had been the case with his last partner.

"Have you figured out the route we're taking?" Wayne asked

Nick.

"And where we're refueling." Nick nodded. "Did you text David?"

"Of course." Wayne rolled his eyes. "He's alerted the closest field office and there should be a car waiting when we get there."

"Excellent," Nick said. "What about the local LEOs?"

"He said he contacted the local police. They're expecting us, but he didn't give them specifics. He was concerned that maybe there might be another incident like Yarnell."

"And the seminary?"

"He just told the locals there that we were looking for Clarke because he was the last to be seen with a victim." Wayne shrugged. "The local field office there knows the real reason, as does the one in North Dakota."

"As long as Clarke doesn't run again," Nick said.

"He won't," Sara told him. "This is what he wants—a showdown between him and me on his 'home turf', as it were. He has some kind of advantage there."

"What kind of advantage?" Wayne asked.

"I won't know until I get there." She shrugged. "But it has to have something to do with my gift, of that I'm sure."

"So maybe something bad with the earth then," Wayne suggested.

"Perhaps." Sara relaxed into the seat and looked at Nick. "You going to try to beat your record to Logan?"

"The sooner we get airborne, the sooner we get there."

"I hope you planned a mealtime during our journey," Sara told him. "My breakfast was light and already half-way gone."

Nick frowned.

It was obvious to Sara that he hadn't thought about feeding her or Wayne. The feeling she was getting from him was consternation as if he had did something majorly wrong by not doing so.

"I'll get us something when we refuel."

Wayne looked at Nick. "You can starve me but you better take better care of her."

"It's alright." She laid a hand on Nick's arm. "You're not used to this. I get it."

This connection they had was getting stronger and she was getting to the point of being able to read his emotions more readily.

At least she wasn't feeling them, and they were still faint, where she could ignore them if she wanted to. She wouldn't have been able to handle it if the emotions coming from Nick tried to overwhelm her own.

A hand covered hers and squeezed before returning to the steering wheel. Relief and affection was 'radiating' from Nick now. Sara could get used to this; feeling all these positive emotions toward her from him. It might even help with her gift. With his emotional support she wouldn't have to worry so much about being overwhelmed by strong negative emotions at a crime scene or on 'bad' land.

Nick pulled into the airport, heading for outer edge where the hangers for the small private planes were. "Did you text the local office?"

"Yeah. They're going to park the SUV in long-term parking for us in case we have to come back." Wayne paused. "They're also going to keep an eye on Yarnell."

"Good."

Three hangers came up on the left with several planes parked on the tarmac before them, and Nick pulled up next to the second hanger where a plane sat in the open doorway.

The plane was a bright yellow with black numbers on the tail, and didn't look to be able to hold all three of them and their luggage. At least not to Sara's eyes.

"I have to go and file a flight plan." Nick gestured to a small shack Sara hadn't seen until then. "You can wait here. I won't be long."

"I can load the luggage while you do that," Wayne said before sliding out of the SUV and moving to the back of the vehicle.

"You still have that bad feeling?" Nick touched her cheek.

"Yes." She leaned into his touch.

"Nothing's going to harm you as long as I can help it." He ran his knuckles down her cheek before turning and opening the driver's door. "I'll be back in a few minutes."

Sara watched him walk to the shack. Her foreboding only increased the closer they got to North Dakota.

Clarke was there and he was waiting for them. For her.

CHAPTER FIFTEEN

"Sara."

Her name jerked her awake, and the vague dreams receded. She had fallen asleep just after they left their refueling stop so they must be at their destination by now.

Nick, sitting in the pilot's seat next to her, turned towards her. She glanced back and noticed Wayne looking at her as well.

"What?" she asked.

"You were twitching," Nick told her. "And I called your name a few times."

She frowned as she thought about the vague images. They could have been premonitions or just impressions from the Aether. "I was dreaming."

"Were they just dreams?" Nick frowned.

"I don't know." Sara shook her head and straightened as she caught sight of two vehicles headed their way. "We'll talk later. We've got company."

The other two glanced out the window, then both nodded agreement.

Sara opened her door and slid out of the plane. She was grateful for the asphalt under her feet. More charged energy right now would just be too much.

Nick exited and stood next to her while Wayne pulled out their bit of luggage.

The two black SUVs drew to a stop in front of Sara and Nick, and a man in a suit got out of one of them. He tossed a set of keys to Nick before speaking. "I'm Agent Jameson."

"I'm Issaro and this is our consultant Sara Phillips," Nick said. "Have you found any sign of Clarke yet?"

"He rented a car here," Jameson told him. "But we haven't been able to locate him."

Wayne moved past them and put the pile of luggage into the SUV before coming back to join the other three.

"You made arrangements for us." Nick's tone made it a statement, not a question.

"There's a map and directions to both your hotel and the police station on the front seat." Jameson paused. "I also wrote down directions to Clarke's old family home."

"Anyone living there?" Nick asked.

"No, and it's outside of town. We figure he might be in the woods surrounding the place. Lots of places to hide."

"You have people watching the place?" Wayne spoke up.

"A pair of agents are staying there. We didn't want to involve the locals that far."

"Good thinking," Nick said. "We're going to go to the family home before we retire to the hotel."

"Alright." The agent pulled out a cell phone. "I'll let the men there know to expect you."

Nick gave the agent a nod, then escorted Sara to the SUV with a hand on her back. He helped her into the passenger seat before he moved around to the driver's side.

"Is there a reason we're headed toward the family home instead of dropping off our bags first?" Wayne got into the back seat as Nick slid into the driver's. "It's not as if we know for sure he's there."

"I want to look at the playing field." Nick picked up the map lying on the seat next to him and glanced over it. "And give Sara a chance to 'read' the land before we engage Clarke."

"He wanted us here for a reason." Sara looked back at Wayne. "Something made him choose this as his standing ground."

"There's a note here that there's an old cemetery not far from the house." Nick tapped the piece of paper attached to the map.

"But it doesn't say whether it's family or public."

"Depending upon age, it could be both," Sara told him.

Nick grunted and handed the map to Wayne before starting the SUV. He gave the still waiting agents a wave, then drove across the tarmac.

"What's the worst case scenario?" Wayne asked Sara.

"There's a couple of ways this could be bad for me." Sara turned her head and stared out the window. "Death releases massive negative energy which the earth absorbs and if the earth is already 'bad'…"

"Bad?" Nick's right hand moved and grasped her left, giving it a squeeze. "I thought Mother Nature was benign."

"For the most part the Earth is." Sara paused and turned her hand to grasp Nick's back. How to explain this? Simple would probably be best. "But nature is also what we would call cruel. Natural selection, survival of the fittest, the needs of the many outweighing the needs of the few, type of thing."

"I get it." Nick squeezed her hand again. "So some places are more harsh than others."

"Yes."

"So if a lot of death occurs in these places, it gets worse?" Wayne leaned forward. "Or would only a sensitive know it?"

"Not only sensitive. Bad things happen in those places more so than in others."

"But it will be worse for you." Nick's tone made it a statement.

"Yes." Sara turned her head to look at Nick. "As soon as I step out of the vehicle, I'll be hit with the energy."

"The emotion." Again his tone made it a statement.

"Yes."

"You think that's why he came here." Wayne spoke in the sudden silence.

"If his mother was gifted, then he would know what would happen to me when I came here."

"What exactly could happen?" Wayne leaned between the seats. "Would there be physical signs like fainting?"

Sara snorted. There would be signs alright.

"I gather it would be more than that." Wayne commented when she didn't continue right away.

"The least it could do is make me sick or have a panic attack, the worse…Well, I could technically die or go into a coma."

Nick's grip tightened on her hand and she gave him a reassuring smile, squeezing his hand back. That last was unlikely since she was healthy and young. Sickness, age, and infirmity weakened one's life force and made it easier for the negative energy to overwhelm the life force. However, Voices also had natural defenses against the negative aspects of their element so they rarely succumbed completely.

"Is there any way to test the land without risking that?" A worry line appeared on Wayne's forehead as he frowned. "Seems there should be."

Before Sara could speak, Wayne grabbed the seat to keep from bumping into her and flying forward. The road they were on had suddenly turned to gravel and Nick had touched the brakes.

"Sorry." Nick glanced at Wayne as they continued at a much slower rate. "You okay?"

"Once my heart gets out of my mouth," Wayne told him. "We should almost be to the family home."

"I can see the turn off ahead."

Fields of what looked like hay surrounded them and extended ahead, but ended at a tree line that began about an acre in from the road on both sides. Two houses sat ahead on the left before the road disappeared over a hill while only one house sat at the tree line on the right. An SUV sat in front of that lonely house and Sara guessed it must be the family home.

Nick slowed and turned. The turn off continued on into the woods, but he pulled up alongside the other SUV. He shut off the vehicle and they all stared at the building.

The house was a traditional two story farm house with a large front porch. Paint was peeling off and there were some boards missing, but it looked good for an abandoned house. Sara could picture a little boy playing here, even now.

"How do you want to do this?" Nick still held her hand and gave it another squeeze.

"Come around to my side and open the door." She loosened her grip and allowed Nick to withdraw his hand. "Be ready to catch me if I 'faint'."

Both Wayne and Nick got out, and Nick moved around the

vehicle while Wayne stayed by his door. Nick opened her door and held out a hand to help her from the SUV.

Sara twisted in her seat and took the hand before cautiously sliding out of the vehicle. Negative energy went through her the second her feet touched the ground. Luckily her shoes muted the intensity or she would have indeed fainted. Her hand tightened on Nick's and he pulled her into his arms.

"Are you alright?"

His energy surrounded her, muting the negative, and she regained her equilibrium. She gave a nod against him, but didn't otherwise move or speak. The land was reeking of death (and what humans would call evil), and she was still sorting through what she was receiving.

"Elliot, go inside and talk to the agents," Nick told Wayne. "Sara and I will stay here for the moment."

"Alright." Wayne touched Sara's shoulder lightly before heading toward the house.

"Can you tell me what you've got?"

"Death and blood." Her voice was muffled against his shirt. "Fear, terror really."

She felt Nick tense and his arms tightened around her. However, before she could say anything, there came a familiar presence or rather a familiar 'absence'.

Clarke was here.

But it wasn't his voice that greeted them.

"Hello, Nick."

Another presence came into her extended aura's sphere and by the voice Sara knew it to be Yarnell. From Nick's reaction of tightening his arms around her, she figured Yarnell had a pistol. Sara turned her head slightly and saw the woman. The former cop had obviously come from the house so there would just as obviously be no help right now from that quarter.

"What happened to Elliot and the other two agents?" Nick spoke in a calm voice as if there was not a gun on them.

"The two agents are dead." Clarke was the one who answered him, not Yarnell, as he joined them by the SUV. He was wearing black robes this time instead of what he had worn at the church. "We took care of them when Olivia arrived."

"I knocked your partner unconscious," the former cop said.

"And tied him up."

"He should wake in time to greet the other agents when they arrive." Clarke pulled out his own pistol, an older model revolver. "I'm sure you realize that we have silver bullets in these guns."

"Obviously." Nick's tone was contemptuous.

"Sara and I are going to take a walk one way, and you and the detective are going another."

Nick's arms remained tight around Sara. Anticipation was sweeping through her, equally from Nick and the land. Both knew something was going to happen momentarily.

"Why don't we kill them both right here?" Yarnell's face was full of hatred.

A gunshot rang out but it was not aimed at either Sara or Nick. Yarnell was the one who dropped to the ground, her head a bloody mess. The violent energy soaking into the ground along with the blood from that death made Sara shudder, and Nick's arms tried to pull her impossibly closer.

"It would seem I'm going to have to take you both," Clarke's voice was calm as if he had not just shot someone.

"Why did you shoot her?" Nick's voice was equally calm.

"Same reason I brought her here; she was a liability." Clarke motioned with the pistol. "Please follow the road into the woods."

Nick kept one arm wrapped around her as he turned both of them to do as Clarke said. "Killing us will not help you."

"Nothing can help me," Clarke said as he moved to follow them "But she can do something that will help the land."

"I'm not a shaman," Sara denied. "And my death will only re-enforce the curse here."

"You lie," Clarke almost growled. "Mother said sacred blood will cure the land."

"I'm not a shaman," she reiterated.

"We shall see." Clarke stayed just far enough behind them that they couldn't jump him, but close enough so they couldn't get away without him shooting one or both of them.

"Where are we going?" Nick's tone was calm.

"The cemetery." Sara answered for Clarke when he remained silent. "For any truly big earth ceremony you have to have a bit of 'holy' ground, even if it's tainted."

"He plans to use you as a sacrifice." While Nick's tone was

still calm, Sara could sense the turmoil of emotions within him. "He thinks that will cleanse the land."

"A shaman can perform a ceremony that can cleanse the land, but what he plans to do is completely different." She paused as the trees closed in around them. "He has the erroneous belief that my death will renew this land."

"Your blood will renew this land."

"I keep telling you I'm not a shaman." She was tired of saying this.

"You walked the other side."

"It takes more than that to be a shaman." Visiting Death's realm did not make one a shaman, only a sensitive, though it was one step towards being one.

The road ended ahead in a small graveyard cul-de-sac with a bit of clearing around the dozen or so graves. Each of the graves was an equal distance apart, and the whole graveyard was laid out in a circular fashion with radiating stone lines. Sara recognized the shape immediately, but kept silent for the moment. No wonder Clarke—and his mother—were obsessed with shamanism.

"Stop right there." Clarke spoke as soon as Nick and Sara came to the first grave.

Both turned and looked at Clarke who had stopped a few feet back. Nick kept his arm around her, and Sara leaned into him. She knew what was coming next.

"You really think 'blood magic' will work," Nick said. "It's been scientifically disproven."

"By a Vampire." Clarke glared at Nick. "You vamps have a vested interest in disproving it."

"Don't tell me you believe in that conspiracy crap too." Nick shook his head.

Sara knew he was just buying time but she also could tell that Clarke wasn't going to be sidetracked or stalled for long. His obsession was too deep.

"Sara, please go to the center cairn." Clarke kept his pistol pointed at Nick. "Or I will shoot Agent Issaro."

Nick's arm tightened, and he turned her until she was resting with her head against his chest. "She's staying here."

Anticipation shot through her again from Nick and the land. A presence tickled the edge of her extended aura's sphere, but she pushed it away and closed her eyes, absorbing Nick's essence instead. Energy flowed through her and she clung to him, overwhelmed. She barely heard the cocking of the pistol over the roar of her rapidly beating heart.

Down!

Nick and Sara dropped at the same time as the shot rang out.

Nick twisted at the last second so he landed first with Sara on top of him. He immediately rolled until his body covered hers, but Sara barely felt his weight.

Energy was still roaring through her bond into the land, and she was only just holding her own against the rush. The land was almost babbling to her about all the things that had happened in the past on this bit of earth.

She felt a familiar presence fully enter her extended aura's sphere. That intrusion broke her clear connection with the earth and allowed her to come back to the present.

CHAPTER SIXTEEN

He wasn't a bad boy, the land whispered in her mind. *Despite his wrongness.*

"Are you both alright?" came the familiar voice of the sheriff as the earth went silent.

Neither answered as Nick moved off Sara and stood, holding out his hand to her. He helped her to her feet, then turned to look at the sheriff kneeling beside Clarke's crumpled body. "He alive?"

"No." the sheriff lifted his hand from Clarke's body and shook his head before standing and holstering his weapon. "There's not a lot of blood."

"He was dead before your bullet hit him." Sara allowed Nick to pull her into his arms but she kept her eyes on the sheriff. "What are you doing here?"

"That's a fine thank you." Jacob smiled but there was no humor in it, more of a baring of teeth, the canines of which were pointed. "I came after I found out Yarnell was missing. A check of her phone records showed an out-of-state call before she disappeared."

"So you decided to break cover and come here?" Sara frowned at him. The fact that Jacob was a vampire was not common knowledge in or outside his county. Politics and government was still somewhat verboten to vampires, though many hold assistant

144

jobs to several human politicians and worked in government offices. Vampires that worked in law enforcement above a certain level had to be open and registered to ensure there was no special advantage given.

"No one's going to realize what I am, Sara."

"Let's keep it that way. Clarke and Yarnell have caused enough trouble."

"You said he was dead before my bullet hit him." The sheriff looked down at Clarke. "What did you mean?"

"And who told us to get down?" Nick gripped her chin and raised her head so he could meet her eyes. "It was in my head."

Sara wasn't sure how to explain or even if she would have time. Agents from the FBI were no doubt due anytime now, and they really should get back to see if Elliot was alive.

*Tell him...*came the whisper across her mind.

"I don't know where to start."

"I could feel that you had merged yourself in the link," Nick told her. "Then I felt as if I was shot full of adrenaline. Seconds later, that voice told us to get down."

"You know that all living things have a connection to the earth. That they come from the earth and return to the earth."

"You told me that vampires have a better connection," the sheriff said. "And that's how you can tell a vampire from a regular human."

"Not necessarily 'better', just more direct. Vampires have touched the Aether through their earth link due to their condition."

"That voice was the earth?" Nick continued to look into her eyes. "Is that what you hear all the time?"

"More like whispering usually unless I lay my hand down."

"I can see where one could go crazy." Nick released her chin and ran his fingers down her cheek.

"That explains what he 'heard', but what about Clarke?" the sheriff asked. "What happened to him?"

"He was a Sinq." Sara turned her head to look at Jacob better. "The earth abhors a vacuum. I think if it hadn't been for his mother he would have been dead a long time ago."

"That still doesn't tell me how he died."

"An autopsy will probably say an aneurism of some kind, but the land took him 'home'."

Running footsteps came from the dirt road, and all three turned their heads to see two armed men appear. The men stopped at the sight of them.

"I'm Agent Issaro," Nick told the men. "What's the situation at the house?"

Both men holstered their weapons, and the taller of the two moved to join the three of them. "Agent Wayne is nursing a headache, and Agents Grayson and Taylor are dead. Detective Yarnell was alive when we arrived, but died minutes later. An ambulance is on its way, and we have more agents at the house."

"The dead man's Clarke." Nick gestured to Clarke's body. "He and Yarnell ambushed us at the house."

"That's what we figured," the agent said. "We noticed the footprints on the road and decided to follow."

"Go back to the house and call in CSU," Nick ordered. "I'll wait here for them."

"Right." The agent moved away. "I'll be back soon."

Nick watched that agent walk away, then looked at the sheriff. "I want you and Sara to leave before CSU and the others get here. Go to our hotel, the Fremont on Scenic."

"Leave a crime scene," the sheriff commented with a raised eyebrow. "Before we give our statements?"

"I'll take care of it."

Sara could sense apprehension coming from Nick, but she couldn't tell about what. She raised her head and met the eyes he lowered to look at her. His eyes and face gave nothing away, and she frowned at him.

"It's better all around, Arressa." He cupped her cheek and ran a thumb across her lips. "Don't be upset with me."

"As much as I hate to break this up." The sheriff's voice interrupted the spell Nick seemed to be trying to weave. "But we need to leave."

"Right." Nick removed his hand from her face and took a step back. "Go to the hotel and wait for me there. Both of you."

"Alright." She could sense the longing, regret, and determination in him, along with an emotion she couldn't name.

"I'll go straight there when I'm done here." He made a cross, then held up his hand in the scout sign.

Sighing, Sara turned and went down the road past Jacob who

146

moved to walk beside her. "Where'd you park?"

"Behind the SUV. I was only a few minutes behind you at the airport."

"I'm not going to ask you how you got here so fast." Sara sighed tiredly. "I just want this day to be over with."

A pair of agents walked by them, and Sara and Jacob sped up their pace. They made it to the vehicles, and slid into Jacob's sedan before they heard yelling. Jacob started the vehicle and headed toward the main road at a fast clip.

"Is Nick going to be in real trouble over this?"

"Not over you," the sheriff said as he pulled onto the main road and headed back toward the city proper. "The law is lenient about vampire mates, and the actions of vampires about them."

"So you'll be the one they question him about then."

"I'm sure he can handle it." Jacob paused and glanced at her. "Have you told him anything about your past yet?"

"I'm just as sure he had Elliot to do a background check on me the day he met me."

"That's not the same and you know it. He's not going to leave you, Sara."

"He said we'll take some time after this case." She stared out her window. "I don't know if I can go through it again."

"It will be fine, you'll see."

"I don't know why I'm taking relationship advice from you."

"Beks and I have an understanding." By the tone in the sheriff's voice, Sara could tell he didn't want to discuss this. "Vampires have a different outlook on relationships."

"I know mates are different than companions, Jacob."

"But I don't think you really get it." Jacob exhaled heavily. "There are genetic, emotional, and mental changes when a vampire is mated. Everything is geared to keeping the mate happy and interested."

"I know that a bond is established, but what changes?"

"Agent Issaro should be explaining this to you."

"I know you're not shy." She turned her head to look at him. "So there's got to be another reason you don't want to talk about this."

"All I'm going to say is that he won't leave you. He can't."

"Jacob..."

"I'm not saying anything more about this. Talk to your mate."

She looked at him for a minute longer, then nodded before turning to stare out her window again. "Alright."

Both of them remained silent as the sheriff navigated the city streets to the hotel. Jacob parked close to the front entrance, and they both got out.

The hotel was a two story colonial style building, and white columns stood on each side of the covered entrance. Office buildings were on both sides of the hotel; one of which advertised a café inside.

"Do you want anything?" The sheriff gestured toward the café sign. "We may be waiting awhile."

"Not right now." She headed toward the door, and the sheriff fell in step with her. "You think it will be a long time before Nick and Elliot will be done?"

"Depends on whether they decide to do a full debrief tonight or wait until tomorrow morning when they have evidence from the scene." The sheriff opened the front door when they came to it, and followed her in. "This is nice."

There was a desk set before them along the staircase while the rest of the lobby was set up like a Victorian-era parlor. A man in a blue blazer stood at the desk and greeted them as they approached.

"Welcome to the Fremont. I'm Dan. How may I help you?"

"I'm Sheriff Jacob, and this is FBI consultant Phillips." The sheriff paused to allow the clerk to absorb what he said. "I believe there are rooms held for Agent Issaro."

"Yes." The clerk tapped on the computer beside him. "Agent Issaro called and told us to expect you."

"Excellent." The sheriff held out his hand for the key. "Did he say anything else?"

"Just that he'll be here as soon as he can."

"Alright." Jacob took the two keys from the clerk. "The room is upstairs?"

"Yes, room 204."

"Thank you." The sheriff gave the clerk a nod, then followed Sara up the stairs.

Their room was the second door on the left, and they hurried inside. A queen-sized bed took up most of the room, but there were two chairs and a table by the window. The bathroom was just inside the door to the right, just big enough for the necessities. Everything was in various shades of blue, including the carpet and curtains.

"I wonder if the other room's like this?"

"Probably, though maybe a different color." Sara moved to the bed, and sat down. "Well, the mattress is firm."

The sheriff merely raised an eyebrow before moving to sit at the table.

"You said you came after Yarnell disappeared. How did you know she was gone?"

"I thought you weren't going to ask me how I got here so fast."

"Is it related?" Sara scooted back until she was leaning against the headboard and pulled her legs up onto the bed. She needed to talk, to keep from thinking about what had happened earlier. At least until Nick returned.

"Sort of. I was at the police station when they became aware that Yarnell had slipped her leash, so I had them request her phone records. As soon as I saw the out-of-state call, I realized where she must be headed." Jacob paused as he shifted, stretching his legs out. "I acted accordingly."

"And possibly exposed yourself to potential trouble."

"The government's been ignoring our frays into politics for decades." Jacob made a little wave with his hand. "I doubt a vampire sheriff is going to tip the scales. The town council on the other hand, might be in for a bit of trouble as two of them are vampires. Luckily the mayor's human and on our side."

"And the city is virtually all vampires anyway."

"There is that too." The sheriff smiled. "It will be okay, Sara."

"I hope so." Sara rubbed a hand over her face tiredly.

"Why don't you take a nap?"

"I'm afraid of what I'll see if I sleep right now." Sara drew her knees up and put her arms around her legs. "That land was bad."

"Worse than a crime scene?"

"Lots of death had happened on that entire land for centuries."

"I thought your gift was limited in scope." The sheriff looked at her. "That you had a 'sphere' of reading."

"I told you that I had a 'sphere' around me, and it was through it that I read things."

"Okay…"

Sara could tell he still wasn't getting it. "Think of the 'sphere' as my aura and you'd be closer. That's how I can read even through clothing and shoes; it touches the earth. I can read any energy caught in the earth that is within the area of my aura, and 'hear' echoes of energy past it."

"What about the earth talking to you?"

"Oh, that's completely different." Sara made a little motion with her hand. "It's what makes me a voice instead of what we humans would term a psychic, though it too uses my aura."

Jacob's phone rang, and he pulled it from his belt.

"Hello." He paused for a moment, then spoke again. "Alright. See you soon."

"Nick?"

"Yes. He said he's on his way." Jacob put his phone back on his belt. "It seems they're done with him for now."

"I suppose we'll have to give statements tomorrow morning."

"I will at least." Jacob shifted in his chair again. "Depending on what Nick has told them and what they find."

"Well, an autopsy will show he didn't die from your bullet."

"I don't know if that's a good thing or not." Jacob paused as he frowned. "They might get in their heads that you caused his death. You being psychic and all."

"Technically, I am responsible, I suppose."

"He was the one who chose this place, not you," the sheriff reputed.

"True enough." Sara rested her head on her knees. But that didn't mean she wasn't still responsible. "He had the erroneous belief that my blood would 'cure' the land."

"Blood 'magic'." Jacob shook his head. "Even with modern advances, humans still believe in superstition."

"Well, blood magic's not complete superstition."

"What?" His eyes darted to her as he raised an eyebrow.

"When you consume blood from a live person you get their emotions with it, do you not?"

"But that's the chemicals." He protested. "Hormones."

"You are consuming a part of the person's life force," she told him. "That energy leaves after a time when removed from the body, the source. A true shaman can use that energy for what could be termed as 'magic'."

"Our scientists are trying to dispel many of the paranormal myths about us." Jacob had a thoughtful look on his face. "Perhaps that is one that has a grain of truth to it."

"Perhaps." Her stomach took this time to growl, and she grimaced.

"How about I get some food from the café?"

"I guess I should eat," she conceded.

The sheriff laid one of the keys on the table, then stood. "I'll lock the door behind me."

"Clarke's dead."

"Doesn't mean there's not someone else." Jacob moved to the door and opened it. "I'll be back as soon as possible."

"I'm not going anywhere."

"You better not."

Sara watched the door close behind the sheriff, then closed her eyes. She had a lot to think about.

CHAPTER SEVENTEEN

Nick and the sheriff showed up at the same time. Sara was still deep in thought when the door opened to reveal the two vampires. The sheriff went to the table with the food while Nick moved to sit on the bed beside her.

"Are you alright?" Concern radiated from Nick.

"Just thinking," she reassured him.

"You're sad." He cupped the side of her face and ran his thumb across her cheekbone. "Tell me what you're thinking about."

"Today." She wrapped a hand around the wrist near her face, her fingers touching the pulse point. "So much death."

"They brought it upon themselves," the sheriff spoke up.

"I know, but it was still a waste." She paused as her stomach growled. "What did you bring me?"

"A burger and fries."

"Comfort food, excellent." She gave the sheriff a smile. "I'll eat at the table."

The sheriff grabbed the second bag he had set down, and moved toward the door. "I'll stay with Agent Wayne tonight and keep an eye on him."

"How is he?" she asked.

"Concussion, but otherwise fine." The sheriff opened the door.

"I'll see you at breakfast."

The door closed behind him, and Nick stood. His hand dropped from her face but remained extended to help her to stand. He followed her to the table, and sat in the other chair after taking off his suit jacket.

"What happened at the crime scene after we left?" She sat down, and opened the bag of food. "Did you get into trouble?"

"Not really." Nick waved his hand dismissively. "The sheriff will have to make a statement tomorrow, but everything was fine when I left."

Sara pulled out her burger and fries, and started eating.

"You're still sad."

"And I will be for a while." She realized that she had had no control over what Clarke did, but she still felt responsible. Emotions were not ruled by logic.

"Then perhaps I should do something to take your mind off what happened." He leered at her.

"After I finish satisfying my hunger, we'll satisfy yours." She flashed him a smile before continuing to eat.

"When we are done wrapping up the case, you want to go back to Debow or would you rather go someplace else?"

"What did you have in mind?"

"A nice holiday in Florida. I have a condo on the beach."

"Sounds good to me." She shoved the last bit of burger in her mouth as she paused. "I never learned how to swim."

"I'll teach you." He stood and offered her his hand. When she took his hand, he pulled her to her feet and straight into his arms. "I'm never letting you go."

She laid her head against his chest, then raised her face to nuzzle his throat.

He drew in a sharp breath, then moved them both to the bed. His hand slipped under her shirt and slid along her back until he came to her bra. With a flick of his fingers, he unsnapped it, then glided those fingers around front to cup one breast.

"That's not fair, Nick." Her voice was a little breathless as she patted his covered chest.

"It's easily rectified." He unbuttoned his own shirt, leaving his chest bare, before pulling her tee over her head. "Better?"

"Much." She allowed him to remove both her bra and his shirt before drawing his head down and kissing him. He nipped her lip and she deepened the kiss. Desire shot through her, and she could sense his own jolt of lust. Her hands explored him, running through his hair, massaging his scalp, and roaming his abdomen, causing his muscles to ripple at her touch.

Nick broke the kiss and took a step back, his hands going to his belt. He allowed his slacks to fall to the floor, letting her gaze move over him, before he pulled her close again. He removed her jeans, then pushed her onto the bed. "Arressa."

Sara reached out a hand, and pulled him down to join her when he took it.

He moved her to the crook of his arm and held her tightly against him, his free hand roaming her body, stirring her desire. His hand went between her legs, and she parted them to allow him to settle between her thighs. He slid into her and began to thrust, his lips nuzzling her throat.

Her own hands dug into his skin, causing him to moan. His desire was feeding hers, and she was riding the high.

The pleasure built as they continued to move together. Ecstasy lashed through them, and their bodies, minds, and souls suddenly meshed as though they were one.

As they both passed their peaks, Nick bit down at the conjuncture where her neck and shoulder met, and warm pleasure shot through both of them. Satisfaction made their bodies sag limply to the bed.

Nick rolled to the side and withdrew his fangs, licking the wound closed. He bit into his own wrist and offered it to her.

Sara lapped at the wound for a moment, then allowed her head to drop to the pillow. Aftershocks were still rippling through her, and she could sense Nick was also still on a high.

To close the punctures, Nick licked his wrist before relaxing. He settled his hand on her hip, and laid his cheek against her head, breathing in her scent as he held her close.

"What about our luggage?" She was thinking about a shower and wanted fresh clothes.

"I'll fetch it later or even tomorrow morning." He kept his nose buried in her hair.

"How about now? I want a shower."

"We can shower together." Sara could hear the leer in his

voice. "Then cuddle."

"It's true then that vampires don't have a recovery time."

Nick laughed and rolled away from her to sit up at the edge of the bed.

However, before either of them could say anything more, there was a knock at the door.

With a dissatisfied grunt, Nick grabbed his pants and put them on before heading toward the door. He peered through the peephole, then opened the door.

His body and the door blocked Sara's view, but she heard a male voice ask for her.

"Who is it?"

"My grandfather would like to speak with you," the voice said. "Please may we come in."

There was a familiar tension in the air that Sara recognized. She grabbed her shirt from the floor and put it on before slipping under the covers. "Let them in, Nick."

Nick stepped aside to allow them to pass, then closed the door.

The younger man was in his twenties, dressed in a t-shirt and jeans while the elderly man was dressed in a Henley and overalls. They looked like ordinary people, but Sara knew they were not.

"I'm Dan, and this is my grandfather Charles." The younger man paused as Nick moved to sit beside Sara on the bed. "He's gifted like you."

"And you." Sara wasn't letting him get away with denial.

"She's got you, boy." Charles laughed. "We recognize our own."

Dan's jaw tightened and he remained silent.

"We own a farm near the Clarke's house." Charles continued.

"How can you stand all the negative energy?"

"I could lie and say it doesn't affect me." Charles paused to glance at his grandson. "But it does. Sometimes I explode for no reason. Dan keeps himself closed off, but it still affects him. My wife used to keep me grounded, but after she died…"

"I'm sorry."

"Thank you." Charles lowered his head briefly. "But that's not why we're here. I felt what you did at the cemetery."

"I don't know what you mean."

Charles' eyes flickered over her face. "I see you don't. You did an energy transfer."

"Energy transfer?"

"It is rare. Some of those gifted can link the Aether to this physical plane and pass energy between them. Mainly those with shaman potential have this gift."

"Oh, no. I don't want to be a shaman."

"It is not a want, it is what is ordained." Charles met her eyes. "It will happen if it's meant to."

Sara felt chastised like a little kid and bowed her head. She drew up her knees under the covers and wrapped her arms around her legs.

"It can be a burden, our gift, but there are rewards as well."

"I haven't found any." Sara raised her head. "It's only brought me pain and misery for the most part."

"Working for the law as you are, there are sacrifices." Charles agreed. "But you'll find the bond you share with your mate will be stronger and fuller."

"What?"

"For one gifted as we, there is already a bond that forms with our mate, but with a vampire that bond is indescribable. And if you do become a shaman it may be your saving grace."

"How do you know all this?"

"My family's been gifted through the generations. My grandmother passed on her knowledge to me, and I'm passing it on to my grandson, even if he does have a hard head."

"You'll pass the rest on to him when you go?"

"The rest?" Nick asked

"Being gifted just gives you the ability to read the energy." Sara explained "The voice part is different."

"You must have just gotten together." Charles looked from one to the other.

"We did, but we're going to take some time to get to know one another." Sara met Charles' eyes.

Charles nodded but before he could say anything, Nick spoke. Sara could discern he was leery of what Charles wanted. "You said you came here because you felt what Sara did. An energy transfer. Why would that be of interest to you? Because of the shaman potential?"

"No." Charles shook his head. "She transferred a lot of the

negative energy from the surrounding area away. I wanted to thank her."

"You weren't going to ask her to do it again?" Sara sensed suspicion coming from Nick. "To 'cleanse' the rest of the land?"

"Even a full shaman can't 'cleanse' that land. There's been too much death there. But she's made it better for crops as well as for Dan and me."

"Negative energy can affect crops?"

"Just as much as a poison." Charles nodded. "So thank you."

Sara didn't know what to say. She hadn't done the 'cleansing' on purpose.

"We need to go." Dan shifted on his feet, glancing toward the door. ."Ma's holding supper."

"Yes." Charles clapped his hands together. "And I still have work to do. It was nice meeting you both. Again thank you."

Nick got up and moved to the door, opening it to allow them to leave. He closed it behind them and moved back to join Sara on the bed. "You okay?"

"I don't know."

"Is this shaman business really that bad?" He gripped her chin and turned her head to face him. "Is it?"

"I thought I was going mad just with one voice in my head." She met his eyes. "A shaman has to deal with all four elements."

"Obviously it's possible. And Charles only said it was potential."

"True enough." She sighed and leaned into his touch. "Didn't you mention something about showering together and cuddling?"

"Indeed I did." He gave her a quick peck on the lips before rolling out of bed. "Shall we?"

Sara accepted the hand he extended and allowed him to help her out of the bed.

CHAPTER EIGHTEEN

Jacob and Wayne were already seated at a table when Nick and Sara arrived. It was a small café with about twenty tables and an old fashioned jukebox in the corner. The counter was about half full and only two other tables had anyone at them. Breakfast rush was either over or hadn't come yet.

"How are you feeling, Elliot?" Sara slid in her chair and looked at Wayne as she picked up one of the menus on the table.

"Just a slight headache." Wayne touched the bandage that was barely visible behind his left ear. "I'm looking forward to a good night's sleep, of course."

"I let you have two hours between check-ins," the sheriff protested, smiling.

Wayne grumbled under his breath, but both vampires just smiled and didn't comment.

Sara patted Wayne's arm in sympathy, then looked at the menu. She was hungry yet none of the items interested her.

"Any dreams last night?" Jacob's tone was almost casual, though they all knew what he was hinting at.

"Fleeting ones. Nothing bad really, just vague images." Sara laid the menu back down on the table and looked at the sheriff. "You ready to give your statement?"

"I don't know whether to play the country hick that got lucky or the one who ain't much of a hick."

"I'd play it as straight as you can." Nick paused as the waitress came over. "I don't want anything."

"I'll have the French Toast." Sara knew she had to eat something and that was usually the easiest to get down. "And an orange juice, please."

"The scrambled eggs and bacon with coffee," Wayne ordered.

"I'll just have coffee." The sheriff waited until the waitress left before speaking again. "I don't want to step on any toes."

"They'll be too busy pointing the finger at me to worry about you." Nick waved his hand dismissively. "I'm their problem child this time around."

"Nick..."

"It will be fine, Sara." He touched her lips with a finger. "Don't worry."

He's right," Wayne agreed. "Nick's the Director's 'golden child', though he gives our Section Chief a headache."

Sara gave a nod, and Nick removed his finger. He snagged Wayne's water glass and took a sip, raising an eyebrow at Wayne's mock outraged expression.

The waitress returned with Jacob's and Wayne's coffee and Sara's juice, then went back to the counter.

"I gave Jameson the impression that you were following Yarnell, but lost her at the airport." Nick shrugged. "I didn't want to say too much."

"Well, it's essentially correct." The sheriff took a sip of his coffee. "I worked out my statement, don't worry."

"Good." Nick nodded. "While you give your statement, I have to bring Jameson up-to-date on the case. I only gave him the bare minimum last night."

"No wander they're upset." The sheriff shook his head. "Just for you, I had Becky overnight the case files to the FBI office here."

"I should have thought of that." Wayne lightly smacked himself on the forehead.

"Well, you were injured." Jacob moved his hand dismissively. "Don't worry about it."

The waitress showed up then with their food and set the plates before Sara and Wayne before refilling Jacob's and Wayne's coffee cups. She asked them if they needed anything more and when everyone shook their heads, she moved back to the counter.

Sara smothered her French toast in syrup while Wayne peppered his eggs. They both attacked their food with gusto, wanting to get it finished as soon as possible so they all could get to the FBI office before too long.

"Does that include the files from Logan PD?" Nick looked at the sheriff. "Or just the files we brought?"

"All of it." The sheriff smiled. "Becky was more than happy to get rid of them."

Sara snorted but didn't comment as she and Wayne continued to eat.

"She hates a mess," Jacob explained at Nick's questioning look. "The DNA results came in this morning, and Becky texted me. It seems one of the missing doctors turned up in our dump site."

"The body he brought with him." Sara nodded. She set her fork down on her empty plate. "He had some kind of attachment to her."

Before Sara could comment further, Agent Jameson entered the café. He was still wearing the same suit he had worn yesterday. Pausing, he looked around, then spotting them he came to their table. "Issaro, Wayne."

"Jameson" Nick nodded while Wayne set his fork down silently. "What brings you here?"

"The AIC sent me." The agent shifted as though he was embarrassed. "He wanted to make sure you showed up. He also wants to talk to Ms. Phillips."

"He is overstepping his bounds." Nick frowned at Jameson. "Did you take a taxi here?"

"Yes. I figured I could get a ride back with you."

"You can ride with me," the sheriff offered. "Will you be taking my statement as well or will it be another agent?"

"I'll be taking it." Jameson nodded.

Wayne stood and moved to the register at the end of the counter.

The other three stood as well, but moved with Jameson toward the door. Wayne rejoined them just as they stepped outside.

"We'll see you at the office," Nick told the sheriff before he,

Sara and Wayne moved to the SUV. He slid into the driver's seat as the other two slid in on the other side.

"I wonder what's up with Agent Carson?" Wayne asked as Nick started the vehicle. "He seemed okay last night."

"The autopsy probably came in." Nick pulled out of the parking lot and moved into traffic. "He was less 'okay' than you think. He was just good at hiding it in front of you."

"Good thing I just sent a text to the Director then."

"I sent him a brief one last night."

"We going to stay together when we give the briefing or should I watch the sheriff give his statement just in case?"

"Jacob can take care of himself," Sara spoke up. She could tell that Nick didn't like this Carson agent. He was probably why Nick sent her away yesterday. "I'd rather you stayed with us."

"I agree." Nick nodded. "I don't trust Carson."

"Okay."

Nick pulled into the parking lot of a squat three story brick building. It looked more like a commercial office than the FBI office building. He pulled into a visitor slot and shut off the vehicle.

The sheriff pulled in next to them, and they all got out. Nick motioned to Jameson, and he led the way inside.

Hues of beige dominated the lobby. The walls and floor were different shades of taupe. There was a staircase in the middle and the elevators were behind them while corridors led off to each side with unevenly spaced doors along the way.

Jameson led them to the elevators, and once they were all inside, he pushed the top button. "The labs are on the first floor, but our offices are on the third. The second floor is holding cells and some interrogation rooms."

"Do the labs include a morgue?" Nick asked as the doors closed.

"Yes. Our pathologist actually works for the local police, but is on-call for us."

Nick raised an eyebrow but didn't comment.

A few seconds later, the door slid open. The third floor was similar to the first in that it was colored in shades of beige and had two corridors leading off the entry. However, the corridors ended in large rooms with doors evenly spaced along the way.

Jameson led them down the left corridor into the large room which turned out to be divided by groups of cubicles. "Do you want to wait at my desk or in the conference room while I take Sheriff Jacob's statement?"

"The conference room would be best." Nick gestured to the agents moving about. "That way we won't be disturbing anything."

"Alright." Jameson led them back out into the corridor to a door with an 'in use' sign. He opened the door and gestured for them to enter.

The room was dominated by an oval table that took up most of the room. A blond man sat near the head of the table with files stacked in front of him, and he looked up when they all entered.

"Jameson."

"Graham. This is Agents Issaro and Wayne, and Consultant Phillips. They decided to wait here until the briefing."

"You're taking the sheriff's statement then?"

"Yes." Jameson gestured for the sheriff to leave the room and followed him out.

Graham stared at Sara, and Nick moved to block his view. "Is there something you want to say, Agent Graham?"

Swallowing, the agent shook his head and dropped his eyes to the file in his hand. Sara guessed he had never seen a psychic up close or a vampire's mate for that matter.

Nick and Sara sat at the other end of the table next to each other, and Wayne slid into a seat across from them.

Just as they settled, the door opened again to reveal three men. All three men were dressed in casual suits. One man stayed by the door while the other two moved to the head of the table. The older man sat at the head while the other man seated himself on his left across from Graham.

"Carson, what is IA doing here?" Nick addressed the older man.

"How do you know he's IA?" Carson countered.

"Graham. He tensed when he saw him enter."

"I'm here," the IA agent said. "to ensure everything is by the book."

"Then neither of you will mind me taping this?" Wayne pulled out his phone and set it on the table. "To ensure accuracy?"

Carson tensed but the IA agent shook his head, and Carson

nodded.

"Shall I begin with when we got the news of the bodies at Debow, or when we got to Debow?" Nick relaxed in his chair. "I can start at either place."

"Start when you got to Debow." A glint appeared in Carson's eyes and he looked at Sara. "Especially the part where you acquired an unauthorized consultant."

"She is an authorized consultant with the Kester County Sheriff's office who we were working with."

Sara pulled out a small ID badge from one of her back pockets and held it up.

"She was still not vetted by us," Carson dismissed.

"Neither was the sheriff." Nick countered.

"Touche." The IA agent gestured for Nick to continue. "You made the point."

"The sheriff called her in for a consult at the dump site. When the sheriff sent her home, someone who we found later to be Robert Kirkland took a shot at her."

"Kirkland being the nephew of the serial killer Richard Meyer who Ms. Phillips had helped put away ten years ago?" the IA agent clarified.

"Yes." Nick nodded.

"Okay."

"I put her in protective custody, and hired her as a consultant."

"Nice way of saying you slept with her." Carson snorted. "Protective custody indeed."

"Actually he didn't sleep with me that first night." Sara did not like this man at all. He was obviously a bigot. Whether of vampires or psychics or both, she wasn't sure. No wonder Nick didn't like this man or want her near him.

"But he has slept with you." Carson leaned forward, a glint in his eyes.

Before anyone could answer him, the door opened again and a middle-aged woman walked in with an older man at her side. The woman was dressed in a dress suit while the man wore a polo and slacks.

"Assistant Director Pine, what are you doing here?" Carson straightened in his chair. "I thought you and Agent Ryan were in a meeting."

"Which is why you're having this meeting now," the woman, Pine, said, causing Carson to flush. The older man with her remained at the door next to the agent standing there, while she moved to sit at the table with Nick, Sara, and Wayne. "Please continue."

"Carson wants to confirm that I slept with Sara," Nick told her.

"Vampire mates are excluded from the fraternization policy." Pine looked at Carson. "You do know that. Beside there is nothing in the Regs against consultants and agents getting together."

"It compromises the case," Carson blurted out. "And they killed Clarke."

"I thought he died of an aneurism." Pine raised an eyebrow. "You're saying they caused it?"

"She did!" Carson waved a hand at Sara. "She used something to cause it."

"Daniel?" Pine looked at the man who had come in with her.

"I agree." He looked at Carson. "It may have to be permanent."

"Agent Carson, you are hereby suspended until further notice." Pine spoke formally. "There is a guard waiting for you outside. Lay your badge on the table, then clean out your desk and leave the building within the hour."

CHAPTER NINETEEN

Silence reigned for only a moment at her statement.

"You can't do this." Carson leaped out of his chair and slammed his hands on the table. "They are dangerous, I tell you!"

"You will leave on your own or I will have you thrown out." Pine didn't raise her voice, but glared at Carson. "Those are your options."

"Aren't you going to do anything?" Carson appealed to the IA agent.

"If she has a good reason to suspend you I can't do anything."

"Mental instability," the man, Daniel, said. "Obviously."

"What?" Carson glared at Daniel. "I am not crazy."

"Your actions aren't showing it," Daniel retorted.

"I'm going to take this up with the Director."

"Feel free to do so," Pine told him. "Now I'd advise you to leave before the guard has to drag you out."

Carson glared at her and threw his badge on the table before he moved toward the door. "This isn't over."

"For you it is."

Carson and the other agent at the door left.

Pine waited until the door closed behind Carson and his lackey before turning back to Nick. "The Director says hi."

"I figured he called you." Nick shook his head. "What is with

Carson?"

"He was on his way to a breakdown for awhile." Pine looked at the IA agent. "You have anything to say, Agent Giles?"

The IA agent put up his hands as if in surrender, but didn't say anything.

"Good." The assistant director's eyes went to Graham. "Have you gone through the files, Agent Graham?"

"Yes."

"And your conclusions?" Pine rested her elbows on the table and steepled her fingers.

"I agree that this could be the work of a serial killer." Graham paused. "The signs of the removal of the womb and broken hyoid bone are consistent."

Pine nodded, then looked at Nick. "You got the call from Kester county and responded."

"Yes." Nick nodded. "The remains were only days old so there was a chance he was still there and hadn't moved on."

"And the Sheriff brought in Ms. Phillips." Pine's eyes flickered to Sara, then back to Nick. "She found additional remains at the dump site that were also the work of this killer and helped further with the investigation even though she was being threatened by a stalker."

"Yes." He drew the word out as he repeated it.

"Then I don't see any problem that you made her a consultant officially." Pine paused as the door opened to reveal Jameson. "Agent Jameson, was the interview concluded satisfactory?"

"Quite satisfactory." Jameson entered and moved to Giles, handing him one of the files in his hand before going to Pine with the other. "These are copies of the sheriff's statement as well as Agent Issaro's."

Pine allowed Giles to look over the statements for a few minutes before speaking. "Well, Agent Giles, is everything satisfactory to you?"

"Everything seems to be in order over the shooting incident with Clarke." Giles closed the file. "But I still have questions."

"Do they have to do with the job?" Pine raised an eyebrow as she looked at Giles over her steepled fingers.

"He sent her and Sheriff Jacob away from a crime scene." Giles tapped the file. "They had time to collaborate, to get their stories straight."

"The sheriff spent his night looking after me," Wayne inserted. "Unless you think this is all a conspiracy, and that I'd be a party to it."

"And a conspiracy for what?" Nick leaned forward in his chair. "What do you think is going on here?"

"Should I be having your supervisor making you an appointment with me?" Daniel asked from where he was still standing by the door. "Sounds like you could use some therapy sessions."

"Agent Carson brought up some valid concerns." Giles looked at Pine. "I'm going to make a report stating those concerns but I'm not going to investigate further. Vampire mates are exceptions, as you said, to many rules."

"If you are done, then I would like to send them home after they debrief Jameson. Unless you think we can't handle the wrap-up on our own?" Pine raised an eyebrow again.

"I would like to stay." Giles clasped his hands and laid them atop the file on the table. "If that is all right."

"Suit yourself." Pine looked at Nick. "Please continue."

"All the victims were active in their churches; that was the only thing they seem to have in common so we sent off for church volunteer lists. Sara also found evidence which suggested that the identified victims had had abortions which led us to look for missing doctors. We figured if he was killing the recipients, then he might have killed their doctor too."

"One of the remains recovered at the Debow dump site was a doctor," Graham interjected. "According to the initial report, she had been dead for at least a decade or more and reburied at least twice. Further analysis is pending."

"I think she was his first kill," Sara spoke up. She had listened to the others, but hadn't had anything to add to what they were saying. Really she hadn't known if she should say anything anyway, but this bit she was mostly sure of. "The others didn't give him the same thrill as she had. They were done through duty, she had called him."

"You could be right," agreed Daniel. "The other kills wouldn't have given him the same rush the first one always does."

"We proceeded to the church where one of the Logan victims

went and I smelled an odor I had picked up at both the Debow dump site and the cabin where another body was found. There were only three men present at the time in the church, two priests and a businessman."

"Fathers Mark Clarke and John Martin, and Mr. Arthur Hoss."

"Yes." Nick nodded to Graham when he named the men. "The two priests showed up missing soon after."

"A local detective had called the suspects," Giles interjected. "The same local detective that wound up dead at Clarke's family home."

"You have a question, Agent Giles?" Pine looked at Giles over her steepled fingers again.

"Just stating facts, ma'am."

"Then I'm sure you know Clarke shot her." Pine returned. "After all, I'm sure you read the report."

Giles lowered his head at the rebuttal, but Sara could tell he wasn't convinced of anything. She knew IA was supposed to be naturally suspicious but this guy seemed of the same ilk as Carson.

"Do you have any questions, AD Pine?" Nick leaned back in his chair.

"I wonder about his reasons for the killings."

"He was angry that the women would reject such a precious gift." Sara told her. This part was true, though not the whole truth. "He was raised to the sanctity of life and the seminary re-enforced that."

"I agree with Ms. Phillips," Daniel said. "What I read in the initial report Agents Issaro and Wayne gave leads me to that conclusion also."

"We tried to be comprehensive in our report of everyone's actions last night."

"It was concise enough for now," Pine told Nick. "I look forward to Agent Wayne's complete report."

"Elliot's?" Sara raised an eyebrow.

"Nick never writes his own reports." Wayne smiled. "He dictates, then I put both of ours in the computer."

"But the Director uses yours, Agent Wayne, as the official report." Pine relaxed and allowed her hands to drop to the table. "Agent Carson should be gone now so you shouldn't have any trouble. I told the guard to remain at the front door until he drove away."

"If that is all, then we will be going." Nick stood, then pulled Sara's chair out for her to rise as well. "Elliot will send you a copy of our final report within the next two days."

"As I said, I look forward to it." Pine gave a nod. "Have a good trip."

"Thank you." Wayne returned her nod as he stood.

Nick, Sara, and Wayne left the room, then headed down the corridor toward the elevator. They remained silent the whole trip to the lobby.

The sheriff was waiting there for them. No one else was in sight so Carson had obviously left the premises.

Jacob greeted them with a nod, then said, "I saw a guard escort someone out."

"That was the late Agent Carson." Nick made a dismissive gesture. "You heading back to Debow today?"

"As soon as I can get back to the airport," Jacob acknowledged. "Becky's the only one who knows I'm here."

"Would you mind giving Elliot a ride to the airport?"

"I guess I could." The sheriff raised an eyebrow. "Are you not headed there?"

"Sara and I are going to stay another night here, then fly to Florida."

"You think that wise with Carson running around?" Wayne frowned.

"If he tries anything, it will be the last thing he does." Nick returned.

"Fine." Wayne huffed in seeming annoyance.

The four of them exited the building and went to their vehicles.

Wayne pulled his luggage out of the SUV and put it into the sheriff's car before going back to the SUV. He accepted the recorder that Nick extended. "I still think you staying is a mistake."

"It will be fine."

"I plan to text AD Pine that you're staying in town tonight once I get her number from David." Wayne warned him.

"If it makes you feel better." Nick paused. "I plan to stay at a better hotel tonight."

"One with room service no doubt." Wayne smiled.

"Exactly." Nick smiled back.

"As soon as I get back I'll start on the report. When I'm done, I'll overnight it to your condo in Florida."

"Excellent."

Wayne nodded, then turned his eyes to Sara who was standing quietly next to Nick. "Enjoy the holiday."

"I'm getting the feeling he's a workaholic."

"He is," Wayne acknowledged. "I plan to enjoy the break myself."

"I hate to break this up, but we need to go." The sheriff spoke up from beside his car. "Becky just texted me, and I got to get back to Debow ASAP."

"Right." Wayne nodded as he turned. "Two weeks, then."

"Two weeks," Nick agreed.

Wayne and Jacob got into the sheriff's car, the sheriff giving them a wave before he drove away.

Nick turned to Sara and pulled her into his arms. "What do you want to do?"

"You said something about a better hotel?" Sara gave him a leer. She was looking forward to some time alone with him without a case pending.

He laughed and gave her a peck on the lips before releasing her. "It even has a casino inside."

"Then we can spend a few hours there tonight before and after dinner." Sara moved to the passenger side and got in while Nick slid into the driver's seat. "And we are going out for dinner."

"As you wish." Nick flashed her a smile as he started the vehicle. "That still leaves lunch."

"Yes, it does." She smiled back as he pulled out of the parking lot and into traffic.

CHAPTER TWENTY

Sara waited until Nick had settled against the headboard before she curled up against him, her head resting on his bare chest. "You didn't bite me this time."

"I don't have to feed every time. As long as you drink, is all that matters." Nick pulled up the sheet until it covered her shoulders. "Are you hungry?"

"Not really." He began stroking her hair, and she gave a contented sigh.

"Tell me about yourself, Arressa."

"I know you've read a file on me."

"It is not the same. You know that."

She gave another sigh. Her life was not a subject she wished to discuss, but she knew she wanted to learn more about him. Tit-for-tat as they say. So she decided to get the hard part out first. "I had cancer."

"Your file said you were hospitalized a few times a little over twelve years ago."

"Jack and I had been engaged for six months at the time. He didn't take it well."

"What do you mean?"

"He started going to work early and staying late. Going out with his buddies on the weekends."

"Leaving you to handle everything alone."

"Yes. The treatments made me sick most of the time as well." She closed her eyes as a turmoil of emotion rolled inside her. This part of her past had played havoc on her self-esteem. She'd best get the next part over with. "I eventually had to have a hysterectomy."

"Let me guess, that was the last straw for your fiancé?" His tone was casual as if she had not just revealed a life-changing fact.

"I had gotten the 'gift' not long before during one of my hospitalizations. He called me a freak." She paused as emotional pain flashed through her. "That was the nicest thing he said."

Nick tightened his arm around her and tilted her face up to look her in the eye. "You are perfect just the way you are."

"You're sure you're not upset that I can't give you a child? That I'm not 'normal'?" She knew vampires could get normal humans pregnant, though the children weren't always vampires.

"Male vampires are not wired that way." Nick cupped her face with his hand, and ran his thumb over her cheek. "As long as you are content so am I."

Sara ran her gaze over his face, looking for the confirmation of what he said and felt. He was radiating serenity and sincerity. It really didn't matter to Nick.

"You said you got your 'gift' during one of those hospitalizations."

"My third to be exact." She paused as she swallowed some of her roiling emotions. That had been a tumultuous time, and it still affected her. "I had gotten really sick again, and I was in the ER when this old man who was dying from poison was rushed in. It was just a coincidence that I was there."

"Everything is as it should be." Nick stroked her cheek again. "Had you not meant to receive it, you would not have been there."

"You are probably right." Sara sighed. "As Charles said, what is meant to be will be. I just hope the shaman bit stays a potential only."

"Everything is as it should be," he repeated. "Tomorrow, we will head for Florida, and we can take our time getting there."

"A bit of sightseeing?" She gave him a smile though her eyes were still suspiciously watery from the emotions stirred up.."

"If you like."

She pulled his head down and rested her forehead against his, her fingers tangling in his hair. "I definitely like."

Nick gave a laugh, then pulled his head and hand away. "You are a tease."

Smiling, Sara settled her head on his chest again and wrapped her arm around his waist under the sheet. He had correctly gauged her interest as non-sexual loving and responded accordingly.

"As for the wedding, you may plan it however you like." He resumed stroking her hair. "According to the vampire community, we are already married."

"And my apartment and things?"

"You may keep it if you like." Nick shrugged. "I can have my financial advisor set up a payment plan."

"Financial advisor?"

"You'll meet her and my American lawyer in Florida," Nick assured her, though she was far from assured.

"American lawyer?"

"I have a lawyer in Mexico and in England where I have interests."

"I'm going to need an ibook to keep everything straight." She sighed.

"I doubt that." He laughed. "Anything you want you tell me, and I'll take care of it, how's that?"

"I'm not going to be a kept woman." She tapped him on the hip.

"You deserve to be pampered." He tilted her head up again to meet her eyes again.

"Pampered, I can deal with."

"Excellent. Let's start with the jetted tub in the bathroom then."

ABOUT THE AUTHOR

Tina Riffey always wanted to be a writer. She started with poetry in grade school and moved to stories by high school. Through a series of moves, she lost those earlier stories, but continued to write down story ideas through the years.

This is her debut novel and the first in The Elemental Voice series. Visit the author's blog at www.tinariffey.blogspot.com for updates on the series.

She lives in Springfield, Missouri with her cat. Tina belongs to Ozarks Romance Authors, Sleuths' Ink Mystery Writers, and Springfield Writers Guild.

Made in the USA
Las Vegas, NV
06 August 2022

52819876R00105